"I want you, Li[ly]"

D0284797

From his voice, Lil[y] [realized he was directly] behind her. The heat of his body reached out to her, a line of fire touching her from her shoulders to the backs of her knees.

She shook her head, but couldn't utter a word.

Lowering his head over hers, he put his lips to her temple. The rest of his body did a similar kind of nuzzling. "You're not my type," he said, "still I want you. Can you feel it?"

A little frantic, she nodded.

"Then I would suggest," he continued slowly and with deliberation, "that you make a point not to encourage me. If you let on that the feeling is mutual, I can't promise I won't take you." The last was said against her neck and was punctuated by a slow, sucking kiss that made Lily feel faint. But just when she needed him most, he stepped back.

Furious in her frustration, she whirled on him. "You gave me a hickey!"

"Not this time," he said. More softly, he promised, "Next time."

When **Barbara Delinsky's** twin sons, fourteen years old and in eighth grade, were given an assignment to interview their mother about parenthood, Barbara gave them this advice: "Being a parent is a twenty-four-hour-a-day job that never goes away." Not that she would ever want it to! Pondering the whole idea of how the responsibilities of motherhood affect a woman led Barbara to create the character of new-mother Lily. Exploring the way in which an infant can cause a man to reveal himself led her to tough and tender Quist. Together Lily and Quist—and six-week-old Nicki—make *Montana Man* one of Barbara Delinsky's most thoughtful and moving works to date.

Books by Barbara Delinsky

HARLEQUIN TEMPTATION
218–FULFILLMENT
249–THROUGH MY EYES

Don't miss any of our special offers. Write to us at the following address for information on our newest releases.

Harlequin Reader Service
901 Fuhrmann Blvd., P.O. Box 1397, Buffalo, NY 14240
Canadian address: P.O. Box 603,
Fort Erie, Ont. L2A 5X3

Montana Man

BARBARA DELINSKY

Harlequin Books

TORONTO • NEW YORK • LONDON
AMSTERDAM • PARIS • SYDNEY • HAMBURG
STOCKHOLM • ATHENS • TOKYO • MILAN

Published December 1989

ISBN 0-373-25380-X

Copyright © 1989 by Barbara Delinsky. All rights reserved.
Except for use in any review, the reproduction or utilization
of this work in whole or in part in any form by any electronic,
mechanical or other means, now known or hereafter invented,
including xerography, photocopying and recording,
or in any information storage or retrieval system, is forbidden without
the permission of the publisher, Harlequin Enterprises Limited,
225 Duncan Mill Road, Don Mills, Ontario, Canada M3B 3K9.

All the characters in this book have no existence outside the
imagination of the author and have no relation whatsoever to
anyone bearing the same name or names. They are not even
distantly inspired by any individual known or unknown to the
author, and all incidents are pure invention.

® are Trademarks registered in the United States Patent and
Trademark Office and in other countries.

Printed in U.S.A.

1

HE WAS A COWBOY. Lily Danziger wasn't blinded enough by the falling snow to miss the faint bow of his long legs or the telltale Stetson on his head. Nor was she troubled enough by the worsening weather to ignore his sheer size. He was a mountain of a man, wrapped in a sheepskin jacket with its heavy collar up against the wind, and he was flagging her down.

She'd never picked up a hitchhiker before. It was lunacy. Just the week before she'd read that a huge percentage of hitchhikers were wanted by the law for one reason or another.

She didn't want to consider whether this one was wanted, or, if so, for what, because her predicament was precarious, to say the least. She was miles and miles from nowhere; hers was the only car on the road; the driving was getting more difficult with the thickening snow; and she was growing more worried by the minute.

What it boiled down to, she decided in the brief time that elapsed from when she first spotted the cowboy's waving hands to when she gingerly applied the brake, was that she was willing to overlook the danger of taking a stranger into her car in exchange for the small comfort it might bring. She'd been alone for the past eight months, but that aloneness was totally different from what she felt now. If her car slid off the road, there would be no one to see, no one to hear, no one to help.

Except perhaps this cowboy.

Her sporty Audi came to such a slow and muted halt that she half wondered if it was final. The thought didn't help her peace of mind much. Nor did the fact that the cowboy had begun to lope toward her even before she'd stopped.

He tugged at the door handle, then bent over to peer into the car, gave an impatient knock and pointed to the door lock.

For the space of a shaky breath, Lily hesitated. Up close and half-covered with snow, the man looked even more formidable than he had before. She thought of the risk. Then she pushed it from mind, because she couldn't *not* open the door, she realized. Not in as remote and hilly a spot in a storm like this. For humanitarian reasons alone, she had to let him in. He hadn't had his thumb in the air. He'd been waving her down as though something were wrong. Something *had* to be wrong for him to be out there at all.

Reaching across the passenger's seat, she released the lock, then returned to her side and watched him open the door, toss a duffel bag onto the floor in back, brush the worst of the snow from his jacket with hands that looked half-frozen, then fold his large frame into the seat beside hers. With the slamming of the door behind him, she felt the chill he'd brought in. Casting a worried glance toward the back seat, she pulled her own thick parka closer against her neck.

"Thought you were going to change your mind," he muttered in a voice that came from deep in his chest. He alternately rubbed his hands together and held them out toward the nearby heating vent.

"I almost did," she said, hoping that it would serve as a warning that she was on her guard. She couldn't see much beyond the collar of his coat, couldn't see whether his features boded well or ill. "What were you doing out there?"

"Trying to beat the storm, same as you." He tossed his head toward a point beyond the hood of her car. "I might've made it if I hadn't gone off the road."

She had guessed he'd been dropped there by someone else, since she didn't see his car. "You were driving?"

"Is there any other way of passing through this godforsaken place?"

She thought of horseback, then thought again. "Did you skid?"

He snorted. "Fell asleep at the wheel. My car's nose-down against a tree. There's no hope of getting it back up in weather like this."

Peering harder through the swing of her windshield wipers, Lily finally made out the tail end of a car sticking up in the snow. Its presence vouched for the cowboy's story, and while that relieved her, she couldn't help but stare at the car. It was headed down what looked to be a steep ravine.

"You were lucky there was a tree to stop you."

He grunted. Taking the Stetson from his head, he opened the door again, whacked the snow off the hat, stuffed the hat back on his head and slammed the door. Then he tucked his hands in his pockets and slid a little lower in the seat, looking for all intents and purposes as though he planned to resume the sleep his mishap had disturbed.

To Lily's knowledge, he hadn't looked at her once, which was just fine with her. She didn't need charm and conversation as much as a bodyguard. As out of place as a cowboy was in northern Maine, this one would serve the purpose if she got stuck and needed a push.

Aware that the storm was getting no better, she shifted into gear, carefully pulled back into the center of the road and, gripping the steering wheel with both hands, drove on.

"How long were you out there?" she asked.

He shifted his legs, which were too long for the space allotted them. His voice sounded just as pressed. "Better than an hour."

"And no other cars went by?"

He made a sound that was halfway between a grunt and a dry laugh. She thought he was going to leave it at that when he muttered, "Gotta be mad to drive in weather like this."

Or desperate, Lily thought. She wondered which of the two he was. "Where are you headed?"

"North."

That much was obvious, she thought, and hadn't realized she'd said it aloud until he muttered, "So why did you ask?"

She shot him a short, sharp look and decided that he had a chip on his shoulder, which no doubt accounted for his breadth. And while she wasn't one to tackle chips single-handedly, she'd vowed when she left Hartford that she was going to be strong, and being strong meant sticking up for herself. Though she hadn't had much practice at it, now was as good a time as any to start.

"Because," she said, taking a breath, "I was hoping you'd say you were on your way to Quebec to do something innocent, like visit your mother. From my point of view, that would be preferable to your heading for the Canadian border to escape the State Police or the FBI or the DEA or someone like that."

"I'm not running from the law." He passed off the statement with such utter indifference that Lily believed him.

"*Are* you on your way to see your mother?"

"No."

"A friend?"

"No."

"Then you must be here on business." She wanted to believe it. A business trip was respectable.

"You could say that," he answered, sounding more weary. Tugging his hat low over his eyes, he set his head against the headrest in a silent declaration that he was done talking.

For the time being Lily settled for the little she'd learned. She had her bodyguard if she needed him, though what she needed most just then was to concentrate fully on the road.

She drove on. Ten minutes seemed like twenty, twenty like an hour. The snow continued its steady fall, mounting on the car, the road, the surrounding landscape until things began to blur together. She drove at a slow pace, which was as fast as she safely could, and even then her rear wheels spun out every so often before regaining traction. Her fingers grew tighter on the wheel, then tighter still when a gust of wind rocked the car. Her eyes strained to see the road. She held her breath for long stretches, as though that would enhance her control.

Intermittently she glanced at the man beside her. He seemed to sleep for a while, then waken with a small jolt, then stare out the front window for a bit before falling asleep again. Though she couldn't see much more than his eyes in the narrow strip between his hat and his collar, the way his brows hugged them was ominous.

She wasn't surprised when after the car fishtailed wildly enough to shake him from his sleep, he swore. "Damn car's too light for this kind of travel."

"I'm sorry," she said quietly. "If I'd realized it was going to snow, I'd have taken the dogsled."

Ignoring her sarcasm, he grumbled, "Didn't you hear the forecast?"

"Obviously not."

"So you set out into the woods in the middle of January without a thought to the weather."

"I gave a thought to it. I just didn't know what it was going to be." Not that it would have mattered, she knew. She'd had to get away fast. The weather had been the least of her worries.

"Real smart," he remarked.

Lily was thinking it was a case of the pot calling the kettle black, but she didn't bother to say it. There seemed no point, particularly when driving demanded so much of her attention. If anything, the snow was gusting harder. Her windshield wipers were working double-time, yet the glass never seemed to quite clear.

When the road took a sudden turn, she managed to negotiate it with only a small skid—through which, a nervous glance told her, the cowboy slept. Within minutes she handled another turn, and, to her relief, the car began to descend. She figured the lower altitudes would bring an easing of the snow, and, if not that, certainly a return to some form of civilization. She wasn't asking for a thriving metropolis, just a place to take shelter until the storm passed. She wasn't desperate enough to risk life and limb, yet she seemed to be coming closer to that by the minute.

A small motel would be ideal. In the absence of a motel, she'd happily pay for the use of a compassionate Mainer's spare room. Hell, she'd settle for a gas station, if that was all she'd be able to find. She needed gas, anyway.

Almost incidentally her gaze flicked to the gas gauge. Her eyes widened, then returned to the road with greater intensity. Finding a gas station was suddenly her first priority.

To her dismay there was no sign of a gas station, or any other relic of civilization along the road, and where she would have preferred to coast downhill, she had to keep her foot on the gas to propel the car through the drifts. Worse, with each passing minute, the road seemed to narrow. If she didn't know better, she'd have said she was on a logging road in the middle of a forest.

That was impossible, of course, she told herself. Just to prove it, she fished her road map from a pocket on the door. But she couldn't take her eyes from the road long enough to study it. One false move and she'd find her own car hopelessly ground against a tree.

As though goaded by her thoughts, the Audi suddenly slid sideways on the road. She twisted the wheel in an attempt to stop the slide, but the shoulder of the road had angled. After a glide that was brief and utterly silent in contrast to the uproar inside her, the car came to a jarring halt against a cluster of dense, low-growing pines.

The cowboy awoke with a start.

"No problem," Lily said. Determined to ward off panic, she shifted into reverse and stepped on the gas, shifted back into drive and did the same, then repeated the procedure several times.

"We're not moving," he stated.

"Give me a minute. One of the tires is bound to catch on something."

"Or get buried deeper." He swore, then growled, "Leave it to a woman," and opened his door. "Put it in reverse," he ordered as he climbed out. "I'll push."

Lily was grateful she hadn't had to ask, grateful that he seemed willing to take charge. She readily obeyed him, all the while fighting off the terrifying thoughts that seemed to be rushing headlong her way.

Bracing his hands on the front of her car, the cowboy pushed when she gunned the gas. The car moved a bit, but slid right back to where it had been the instant he let up the pressure. He gestured for her to try again. She did. The car moved a bit more, then a bit more. It was only a matter of

Montana Man

time before they were back on the road, she told herself, grasping at fragile threads of hope.

The next time she stepped on the gas, though, the engine sputtered, sputtered some more, then went dead, and those fragile threads snapped. Nervous perspiration beaded on her nose as she repeatedly pumped the gas pedal. She shifted from one gear to the next, praying that anything else was wrong with the car but what she feared.

The passenger's door flew open. "What in the hell's wrong?"

"Nothing's happening!"

He slid into the seat, bringing the snow and cold right along with him, and promptly leaned sideways to study the dashboard.

Lily shrank into the far corner of her seat and waited for his explosion. It didn't take long.

"God*damn*it!" Straightening, he pushed back his hat, turned to glare at her and said in a voice that was low and threatening, "You're out of gas."

His voice wasn't all that was threatening. For the first time, she saw his face, and a darker one she'd never met. Tension radiated from his features—from the lean line of his mouth, his straight nose, the low shelf of his brow. His skin was bronzed, and there were crow's-feet at the corners of his eyes much as she'd have expected of a man who spent a good deal of his life squinting against the sun. But where she'd always assumed cowboys to be mild-mannered sorts, this one wasn't. His eyes were coal black, even darker than the hair that had escaped from his hat to fall in scattered spikes onto his brow. Those coal-black eyes bore into hers.

"I've been looking for a gas station," she argued in her own defense, "but there wasn't one."

"Surprise, surprise."

"I've been looking for a long time."

"Not long enough. Don't you know to gas up before you hit the back roads?"

"I did. I started with a full tank."

"When?"

"This morning."

"Where? New York?"

"Hartford. And I didn't think I was *on* the back roads. The line on the map was thick and black."

His mouth tightened. "Thick and black. So what did you think you were seeing out here? Superhighway? Didn't you begin to wonder when there weren't any other cars on the road?"

"I assumed that's just how Maine roads are."

He nodded. "You assumed that's how Maine roads are." His voice hardened. "Baby, no main road is like this." He shot a scowl through the windshield. "Where the hell are we, anyway?"

Grateful to have something to do, Lily quickly lifted the map from her lap and studied it. "Here, I think," she said, pointing to a thick black line that undulated through northwest Maine.

"You think wrong," the cowboy informed her, "unless you've managed to cover a hundred miles since you picked me up." They both knew she'd come nowhere near that. "I went off the road right about here." He fixed a lean, blunt-tipped finger on a spot some distance from her thick black line.

"But I wasn't supposed to be there at all," Lily protested. Her voice shrank. "I must have missed a turn."

"You must have missed more than one. That's quite a feat."

"I followed the road. Where it turned, I turned."

"You were supposed to stay on the main drag."

"I thought the turns *were* the main drag. In case you haven't noticed, the visibility's awful!"

"That's because we're surrounded by trees."

He seemed to have an answer for everything. She tried a few of her own. "It's because the storm's worsening. And what were you doing when I made those wrong turns? Maybe if you hadn't been sleeping—"

"Goddamned thing doesn't look like much of a road at all," he decided, ignoring her accusation. He studied what he could of the landscape.

Lily was beginning to tremble. "It has to be. I was following *something*."

"Damned if I know what it was," he growled and speared her with a condemning look. "Damned if I know where we are. Damned if I know how we're gonna be found. You didn't listen to the weather, you didn't get gas, and you didn't bother to stay on the main road. Baby, when you blow it, you really blow it." He sat back in his seat, returning his glare to the window. "Just my luck to be picked up by a spoiled little rich girl."

Lily had never been that in her life. The irony of his thinking it would have made her laugh, if he hadn't followed up with "Fancy car, fancy clothes, fancy face—" he turned his head slowly her way "—and...no...brains."

The tension inside her burst into anger. "I had enough brains to pick you up."

"No brains there. It was a stupid thing to do. You don't know a thing about me. For all you know, I'm a killer."

"If that were true, I'd have been dead by now, and I'm not. So where would you be if I hadn't stopped?"

"In someone else's car, safe and warm and on my way north."

"Or frozen to death by the side of the road."

"It's not that cold."

"Good," she said, raising her head a notch. "Then you can get out of my car and walk. If you're in such a rush to get to wherever it is you're going, be my guest. *Hoof* it. You're not much use to me anyway. You couldn't even push my car out of a rut."

His dark face came closer. "Rut? You call what we're in a rut?"

She refused to back off. "Go on. Get out and walk."

His dark eyes flashed. "You're the one without the brains, lady. Me, I'm a survivor. I don't go out walking lost in the woods in the middle of a blizzard with night closing in."

Her bravado faltered. "Night's not closing in."

"It's dusk."

"No. It's only dark because of the trees."

"It's dusk. Look at the time."

Lily did. "It's not even four-thirty in the afternoon!"

"Dusk *falls* at four-thirty in the afternoon this time of year."

She swallowed. "It can't!"

"You gonna stop it?"

Her mind raced on. "After dusk comes darkness, and once it's dark, we'll be stuck."

"We *are* stuck. When's that gonna sink in?"

She fought it, though her insides were shaking harder. "Stuck in the snow, but—"

"Stuck out here. Lost. Marooned. Isolated. Cut off from the rest of—"

"Maybe you could try pushing again?" she interrupted, begging and not caring that she did.

"But you've got no gas!" he shouted as though he'd decided she was deaf as well as stupid. In frustration, he slammed a fist against the roof. "I don't believe this. I should've stayed with my own car. Better marooned on the road with myself than on some cow path with a woman—" A sound from the back seat cut him off, and he went utterly still. When the sound came again, he glanced sharply around, and when it continued, he managed a low "What in the hell's that?"

Snapped from oncoming panic, Lily was already dropping the back of her seat. When it was as flat as it would go, she climbed over it to the carrier that was safely strapped behind the cowboy. "It's my baby," she said softly and not at all apologetically. If there was one thing she'd done right in her life, it was giving birth to the small bundle that she now lifted into her arms. "It's okay, Nicki," she murmured softly, gently, more calm than she'd been moments before. Settling in directly behind the driver's seat, she eased the baby's snowsuit back from its face and put a slender fingertip to first one side of the infant's tiny mouth, then the other. "Shhh. Mommy's here." The baby quieted like a charm.

Twisted in his seat, the cowboy stared back at her in disbelief. "A baby?"

"Yes."

"You've got a *baby* in this car?"

She shot him a dry look.

His voice rose a notch, horrified, now, as well as disbelieving. "We're stuck in the middle of nowhere, for the night—maybe longer—and you've got a *baby* in this car?"

Ignoring his prediction, she smiled at Nicki. "I do believe that's what I'm holding."

"How can you say it so *calmly*?"

"How can I not?"

"Aren't you worried?"

Her smile was gone when she looked up at him. "I'm terrified. But it won't do any good to let the baby know it—unless you'd like to listen to her scream for a while."

The cowboy dropped a frown to the bundle in pink. "She'll probably do that anyway."

"Not for long. She's a good baby."

"All babies scream."

"She's a good baby," Lily repeated, but no sooner had she said it when the baby began to whimper. "Oh, honey, what's wrong?" she cooed softly. She clicked her tongue several times and began a gentle rocking motion, but the baby's whimpers were soon full-fledged cries.

"She's hungry," he informed her.

Lily turned her back on him. "I know that."

The baby's cries were small, but so was the car. Lily was used to it. Clearly the cowboy wasn't.

"Well, aren't you going to do something about it?" he demanded. His dark eyes looked a little wild. "Don't you have a bottle or something? Christ, you don't even have any way of warming milk! Didn't you think *any* of this out before you left New York?"

"Hartford. I left Hartford."

"Same difference. So what are you going to do about that baby?"

"Feed her," Lily said. Sitting sideways on the seat facing away from him, she pushed aside the layers she'd been unbuttoning, unhooked her bra and put the baby to her breast.

The silence inside the car was sudden and sweet, as was the gentle tugging created by the baby's suckling. Settling the infant more comfortably in her arms, Lily rested her cheek against the velour upholstery. Outside, the snow whipped the world into a wild frenzy, but she closed herself in a small cocoon with her child.

For the longest time the cowboy said nothing. Lily refused to look up, refused to let him intrude on her private time with Nicki. Nor did she want to be made to feel self-conscious. She wasn't in the habit of nursing the baby in front of people, much less strange men. She kept herself safely angled for privacy, and what the position didn't do, the layers of clothes surrounding her did.

Though she wasn't watching, she clearly felt it when the cowboy finally faced forward. He remained silent for a time. She was beginning to wonder what scathing comment he'd come out with next, when he asked, "How old is she?"

His voice was lower, more civil. Responding to that, Lily said, "Five weeks."

After a short pause came a scathing, "How can you subject a five-week-old child to this?"

She knew he was facing front, looking out at the storm. She didn't have to look to feel the wind. "I think," she said quietly, "that we've been through this before. I had no idea the weather was going to get so bad."

"Why didn't you stop somewhere when the snow began to pile up?"

"There was nowhere to stop. I kept thinking that it might be worse if I turned back. For all I knew, the center of the storm was where I'd come from. Besides, I hadn't passed anything alive for miles, so there was nothing to go back to. I figured there had to be something ahead."

"Might've been if you'd stayed on the main road."

Lily didn't respond. She worked her way through the fold-over mitten of the baby's snowsuit and watched the infant's tiny fingers curl around hers. They were so perfect, those fingers, so small, but perfect. So was the little chin, and the button nose, and the soft gray eyes that held hers.

Lily wondered what those eyes saw. The books she'd read said that during the second month of life those eyes would be unfocused when the baby sucked, that the child couldn't actively look and suck at the same time. Lily wasn't sure she believed it. Her baby's eyes were clear, and she could swear they were focused. Of course, it was possible she was simply seeing her own very focused reflection in them.

Her head shot up when the cowboy suddenly opened the door and started to get out. "Where are you going?" she asked quickly.

"I'm taking a look around while there's still some light left." He slammed the door loudly behind him.

"Go ahead," she said lightly, then whispered to the baby, "That's fine. We don't need him in here. Now, if he scouts around and happens upon a bustling logging camp, we'll be forever indebted to him." She gently waved the tiny hand that held hers. "What do you think of that idea, Nicki? Hmm? Sound like an adventure?"

Nicki continued to suck at a steady pace. After a bit Lily looked up and around, searching for sign of the cowboy. But the snow was covering increasingly larger portions of the windows, and, to her horror, the light beyond was indeed growing dim.

For a split second, she imagined the cowboy not returning. She imagined being left alone, totally alone in the woods in the storm with Nicki, and she felt chilled to the bone. A disgruntled bear of a man was better than nothing, she realized.

Swallowing away her fear, she said to Nicki, "Whaddaya think? Think he'll find a logging camp out there?"

Nicki broke the suction of her tiny mouth.

"*Are* there logging camps nowadays?" Lily asked in a deliberate singsong as she raised the baby to her shoulder and gently rubbed her back. "It's the middle of January. Would loggers be working through the dead of the winter? I can't imagine it, but you never can tell." She gave several pats. "He'd better find *something* out there, or we could be in big trouble—"

The baby burped.

"That's my girl," Lily said with a grin and transferred the infant to the cradle of her other arm. Normally she'd have taken a minute or two to play at that point, but she wanted to finish nursing before the cowboy returned.

Nicki began to take her time, though. As her stomach filled, she grew increasingly content—which wasn't to say that she was done. Lily knew from experience that if she forced an end to the feeding, there'd be fussing. That—and a weakening sense of relief—was why she didn't so much as move a muscle when the door opened and the cowboy slid back into the car.

It was a minute before he brushed himself off, another before he fit himself satisfactorily into the seat. Still he didn't speak.

Unable to bear the suspense, Lily finally blurted out, "Did you find anything?"

"Woods," he said without turning.

"No camp?"

Apparently he hadn't shared her fantasy. "Camp?" he asked blankly.

"Settlement. Houses. House, singular."

"No."

Her hopes sank. She looked down at the baby and, for her own comfort as much as the child's began a slow rocking back and forth. "I guess we stay here, then?"

"You guess right." Though his trek through the storm had taken the edge off his anger, his voice remained hard. "Some shelter is better than none. Come morning, when we're guaranteed light, I can go farther looking for help."

"Maybe the snow will have let up by then."

"Maybe."

"Do you think—is there a chance that someone will pass by here?"

His snort was eloquent.

But Lily wasn't quitting. "What if you tried hiking back the way we came? You'd hit the main road and—"

"I'd be lost in the storm long before that."

"Maybe in the morning?" she asked more timidly. She needed something to cling to.

He turned to her quickly, about to speak, then faced front again just as quickly and growled, "How long does that take?"

She knew what he was talking about. She'd felt the same jolt he had when he'd looked back. As irrelevant as it seemed, there was still something about his being a man and her being a woman. "Usually about forty minutes. She's almost done."

"How often does it happen?"

"Every four hours. She goes for a longer period during the night."

Pulling his hat off, he drove a handful of fingers through his hair. "Knowing my luck, she won't this time."

"She will. She has to. And if she doesn't, I'll just feed her more often."

"Great," he muttered under his breath.

Lily studied him. Though the light in the car was growing dimmer by the minute, she could see that his hair was dark and thick and that though it needed a cutting, the last one had been good. He didn't look unkempt. His jacket and jeans, which was all of his clothing that she could see, looked comfortably worn but clean, and he didn't smell of horse.

Okay, so he was embarrassed when she nursed the baby. There were worse things he could be.

Then again, there weren't many worse situations she could imagine herself in. His earlier words came back to taunt her. In a small, discouraged voice, she repeated them. "I really did blow it, didn't I."

He pushed out a breath. "Yup. Too bad you can't fill up this tank the way you do that kid."

Ignoring his crudeness, she turned her attention to Nicki, who was by now clinging to her nipple for the sake of comfort alone, rather than the nourishment. "All done?" she asked softly. Disengaging the baby's mouth, she put the child to her shoulder, alternately rubbing and patting her back until she'd bubbled. Then, righting her own clothes, Lily tucked her close to her warmth.

"Would you turn the car on for a minute, please?" she asked.

The cowboy looked back and, seeing that she'd finished nursing, held her gaze this time. "What for?"

"Heat. I know it'll drain the battery but—"

He looked like he wanted to laugh but wasn't sure how. "You won't get any heat out of this car. Not without gas."

"Sure, I will. Try it. Turn the key."

"If I turn the key," he said in a slow and tempered voice, "The fan will go on. Just the fan. By now the engine will have cooled off. You won't get a thing but cold air, probably colder than what's in here now."

Refusing to believe that, Lily held his dark-eyed gaze. "Try."

"It'll be counterproductive."

"Try anyway."

He did. Within seconds, cold air was blowing from the vents. She had enough time to extend the fingers of her free hand to discover just how cold that air was before he turned off the fan.

"You were right," she said in a small voice.

"Naturally." He faced front.

"Are you always right?"

"Usually."

"No modesty there," she softly told Nicki. "Too bad he fell asleep while I was driving. If he'd been paying attention to where I was going, we wouldn't be in this mess."

"I thought you admitted you were the one who blew it," came the grim voice from the front.

"I think I'd rather share the blame." She felt the weight of responsibility on her shoulders, and if he was going to be arrogant about it, he could just take a little of that weight.

The only problem was that aside from getting nervous about the baby, he struck her as a competent man. There was a firmness to his voice and a directness to his eyes. While she started to shake each time she thought about what lay ahead, he was calmer. Annoyed, yes, and disdainful of her, but calmer. She guessed he was a practical man, and, just then, with the snow blowing and night falling, a little practicality was in order.

"What do we do now?" she asked.

"Nothing."

"We just sit here?"

"And try to keep warm." He turned to scan the back seat. When he had trouble seeing what he wanted, he went front toward the glove compartment. "Have you got a flashlight in here?"

"I . . . no."

He slammed the cover and sat still in his seat. She didn't doubt for a minute what he was thinking. But she'd never in her life had use for a flashlight in her car, and there'd been no way she could have known she'd need one now.

Feeling more inadequate than ever, she asked, "Do you want to turn on the overhead light?"

"Not until we're desperate. The battery will only last so long." He turned to her. "Our major worry is warmth. Since we won't get any from the engine, we'd better start thinking about substitutes. I don't know what you've got stashed back there, or in the trunk, but if you've got anything we can use, we'd better get it now. It's gonna be pitch-black before long."

The thought of things being pitch-black sent a shiver through Lily. She tried to concentrate on all she'd packed into the trunk of the car. "The diaper bag is back here. There are lots of clothes in the trunk—mine, and the baby's."

"Baby clothes won't keep us warm."

"There's an afghan." It was the last thing her mother had made her. She hadn't been about to leave it behind. "And two heavy coats. One of them is a fur." On principle alone, she hadn't been about to leave that behind.

"Ah, the advantages of wealth," the cowboy murmured as he reached for the keys, but Lily stopped him.

"You can only do it from in here." Holding Nicki tightly to her, she came forward, barely managing to wedge open the door on the driver's side enough to flip the trunk release on the side panel. She slammed the door as fast as she could, but not before snow fell into the car. "Hell," she whispered, brushing snowflakes from the baby's face.

The cowboy was already out, wading through the snow toward the trunk. Covering Nicki as snugly as she dared, Lily returned the infant to her carrier and scrambled over the seats after him.

Cold nuggets of snow hit her the instant she got outside, and she sank knee-deep. Without a thought to the fine leather of her boots, she pulled up her hood and, head-down, worked her way to the back.

The cowboy was standing by the open trunk trying to figure out what was where. Within seconds Lily had her hands on the two coats and the afghan, all of which had been tucked around her suitcases. He took them from her and quickly deposited them in the car. Under the faint illumination of the trunk light, they soon had their arms filled with the heaviest and warmest of the clothes Lily had brought.

"Any food back here?" he yelled above the wind.

She shook her head and headed around the car. By the time she'd tossed in what she carried and climbed in herself, Nicki was whimpering again, and Lily knew why. Wet diapers had a way of upsetting even the most peaceful of babies. Pushing aside the clothes she'd been carrying, she set about remedying the problem.

It broke her heart to have to expose the baby's skin to the chill, to see the tiny legs shake and touch the baby's new, paper-thin skin with her cold hands. The darkness didn't help. Nor did the setup in the car, which was a far cry from the convenience of the white wicker dressing table she'd had for the baby in Hartford. Fumbling around when necessary, she worked as quickly as possible, all the while crooning sweet nothings to Nicki and trying not to think that this could be the best it would be for a while.

The cowboy, meanwhile, made several more trips to the trunk. By the time he climbed into the front and closed the door behind him, there was a mountain of clothing on the driver's seat. Lily didn't realize how much he'd carted in until she had Nicki put back together and snugly zipped into her snowsuit.

"What have you *got* there?" she cried.

"Insulation," was his succinct response. He lowered the back of his seat and reached for the baby carrier. "How does this thing come undone?"

"Why?"

He paused in his groping to look at her. Though his face was shadowed, his tone left little to the imagination where his opinion of her intelligence was concerned. "If I can move it, I can get back there and stuff clothes under the window. In case you haven't realized it yet, the longer we sit here, the colder it's going to get. This car may be state-of-the-art chic, but it ain't gonna keep us warm for long without heat. So we need insulation. Understand?"

Lily did and was annoyed at herself for not anticipating what he had in mind. To compensate, she reached down and released the seat belt that held the carrier in place. Once the bulky piece was wedged between the two front seats, she set Nicki in it and began helping line the back window, then the seams of the doors and the front windows with shirts, skirts, slacks and sweaters. She was grateful for the activity. Not only did it warm her up, but it kept her mind off the reality of what was to come.

Too soon, the cowboy muttered, "That'll have to do." Curving his spine to the back seat, he extended his long legs over the lowered front.

Nightfall had further darkened the interior of the car, but Lily's eyesight adjusted to some extent. Sitting back on her heels, she looked around. The afghan, the coats, several sweaters and the baby things were dark blurs on the driver's seat and in the hollows before the two front seats. She dragged the afghan back to where she was, then reached for Nicki. With the child in her arms, she pulled the afghan up chest-high and made herself as comfortable as possible in her own corner of the back seat.

Outside, the snow swirled relentlessly. Lily listened for a bit, rocked Nicki for a bit, tried to imagine the future when she might look back on this experience and laugh. Laughter of any sort was hard to imagine now. Her sense of optimism seemed to be hovering, not sure which way to go.

She glanced at the cowboy. "What do you think?"

He didn't answer at first, and when he did, his voice was low and tight. "About what?" He had his head back and his eyes closed.

"Can we make it?"

"We have to."

"I know that, but can we?"

"If we're lucky."

"Lucky how?"

"If the snow stops before too long. If it doesn't get too cold after that. If someone sees my car and starts wondering—"

"Were you expected somewhere?" Lily asked hopefully. "Will someone be looking for you when you don't show?"

He killed her hope with a short, deep "Nope," turned his head against the seat back and opened his eyes. "How about you?"

She shook her head.

"No one?" he asked.

Again she shook her head.

"What about the kid's father?"

"He's not in the picture."

The cowboy's gaze pierced her through the darkness. "You just got knocked up for kicks?"

"No, I—"

"—had the hots for a married man and didn't stop to think of birth control."

"No, I—"

"—wanted a baby. Didn't want a husband."

"*No*. I *was* married. I'm just not anymore."

"But you have a five-week-old child. Surely the father knows about it and is going to worry when you don't show up somewhere."

"He knows about the baby. But he won't worry. He doesn't know where we are, where we're going or what we're doing. He doesn't want us any more than we want him."

The cowboy stared at her. Lily refused to look away, but she felt as though she were being skewered. Clearly he was wondering what was wrong with her that her husband would divorce her when she was pregnant. It was a typically male way of thinking. Lord, she was tired of it.

"We wanted different things," she finally said when she could take no more of his silent scrutiny.

"So you took the car, the fur and the kid."

"And my clothes. And the afghan my mother made me. And what little was left of my pride." There were other things she'd taken, but she saw no need to enlighten the cowboy further.

"Then this is the big escape?" he asked with dawning awareness. "You're not just off to see someone or take a vacation?"

"It'll be a long time before I take a vacation, and there's no one I want to see," she said and for an instant regretted her forthrightness. But she pushed her regrets aside. Nothing about the cowboy had suggested that he'd hurt her. She had no reason to believe him to be evil.

Of course, he was a man, and she wasn't thinking too highly of men as a group just then. Then again, she didn't have to like him. All she had to do was weather his company until they found a way out of the mess they were in.

The cowboy straightened his head and closed his eyes.

"Are you going to sleep?"

"Might as well."

"Whenever you go to sleep, something happens. First your car went off the road and then—"

"I'm tired."

"You must be, to have fallen asleep at the wheel in the middle of the day."

"I've been up for nearly thirty-six hours straight getting this far."

"Where did you start?"

"Montana."

"Where are you headed?"

He was quiet. Lily wondered if he'd fallen asleep when his voice came to her, deep and slow. "New York, I thought, but when I got to New York, they said Boston, and when I got to Boston, they said Quebec." He yawned. "If I don't find what I'm looking for in Quebec, I'm goin' home."

She was surprised that he'd said as much. He'd been more laconic until then, keeping personal things personal. Perhaps, she decided, he realized the impossibility of privacy in their situation. Or perhaps her opening up had inspired a little in him. Or perhaps it was simply fatigue, doing in his defenses.

Whichever the case, she wanted to take advantage of it. "What are you looking for?" she asked.

But he didn't answer.

"Are you asleep?" she whispered loudly.

"Almost."

"You won't tell me what you're looking for?"

"Not now," he murmured sleepily.

"What if you fall asleep and freeze to death?"

"You'll wake me before that."

"What if *I* fall asleep and freeze to death?"

"The kid will wake you before that."

"What if she freezes first?"

"Wrap her inside your coat and she won't. You've got body heat. Use it."

His suggestion was a good one, particularly since Lily had a canvas carrier tucked into the diaper bag. By strapping Nicole to her chest, zippering her own coat around them both and covering with the afghan and a coat, she stood a fair chance of keeping the baby warm.

Not that she was moving just yet. The baby was happily clutching her finger, and the air inside the car was far from frigid. But it was a good thought for the future.

On its heels came another thought. "Is there any chance of our asphyxiating closed in here like this?"

The cowboy didn't answer.

"Uh . . . excuse me . . . are you still awake?"

"Barely," came the deep, distant voice.

"Did you hear what I asked?"

"Mmm." He paused, then mumbled, "No gas, no fumes."

She breathed a sigh of relief. "That's good."

"I'm goin' to sleep now. Can you keep still?"

Lily wasn't sure she wanted to keep still. Talking, hearing the sound of her voice, hearing the sound of his was a comfort in the dark. But he was exhausted. Thirty-six hours was a long time to go without sleep. She had to respect his needs if she wanted him to respect hers.

"I'll be quiet," she agreed softly. After no more than a minute, though, she said, "What's your name?"

"I thought you were going to be still?"

"I will. Tell me your name first. That way I can wake you before you freeze."

He was quiet for a very long time. Watching him, Lily could have sworn that his eyes were open for part of that time. At the end, though, they were closed and his breathing was low and even. She was about to give up on him when he said, "Quist."

"Excuse me?"

"The name's Quist."

"Quist?"

"Mmm."

She'd never heard anything like it, didn't even know whether it was a first name or a last name, but when she would have asked, he suddenly shifted, turning away from her.

She let him be. It was only fair, she reasoned. Besides, if luck was on their side, morning would come and with it rescue, and she would never need to know anything more than that the man she'd been stranded with for a night in the snow was Quist from Montana.

2

QUIST CAME AWAKE to a strange sound. At least, it was strange until he got his bearings. There had never been a baby in his life, not of the human variety. He'd had his share of experience with newborn calves, colts and fillies, dogs, cats and the occasional bear, but he'd been spared the joy of human squalling until now.

Opening his eyes to the darkness, he looked around, remembered where he was and why, and slowly turned his head. Though the woman had her back to him, the car wasn't large enough to separate them by much, particularly since they were both stretched out from the back seat forward. If he moved his arm, it would brush her shoulder.

He didn't move his arm.

She was shushing the baby, but the baby had a mind of its own and kept crying while she started fiddling under the afghan. Then came the silence, as abrupt as it had been earlier, and Quist knew she was nursing the child.

He wasn't sure why that made him uncomfortable, and he wasn't about to brood on it, but it did.

He hadn't thought she'd be the type to nurse. Nursing babies was for women who were willing to be tied to home and hearth for months, and he wouldn't have pegged her that way. She looked rich. He guessed that her sporty red car was no more than a year old, that her hip-length turquoise-and-white parka had a designer label inside, that her boots were imported, that her pencil-slim jeans cost three times as much as one pair of his functional Levi's.

Besides that, she didn't look hardy enough to nurse a child, let alone give birth to one. Thanks to the bulky parka, he hadn't been able to see much, but what he'd seen looked small. Her face was slender, her features delicate. Her legs were slim. And standing, as she'd done for a brief time by his side when they were digging things from her trunk, the top of her head hadn't reached his shoulders.

There was a fragility to her. He kept thinking about how she'd gone through childbirth only five weeks before. Her body had to still be recovering. And beyond the physical was the emotional. She might be calm with the baby, but she meant it when she said she was terrified. He'd seen it in her eyes, even when she tried to keep her voice calm.

She had every right to be frightened. They were lost in the woods in an area that very possibly hadn't seen traffic in years. If the situation were different, just him and her, they could stay with the car until the snow ended, then bundle themselves up and hike back toward the main road, even if it meant several days' exposure to the cold.

But he wasn't sure how far she'd make it in the snow, and then there was a baby involved. A five-week-old infant couldn't survive exposure like that. So the options were limited and the responsibility greater, none of which pleased him.

He wanted to be in Montana, not Maine. He wanted to be back home on the ranch, which he knew and loved. He worked hard there, but the work made sense. There was an order to it. Emergencies cropped up all the time, but he could deal with them. He could deal with most anything on his own turf.

This was something else entirely. But then, women had always been the bane of his existence. He doubted that was ever going to change.

"Quist?" came a whisper from the edge of the afghan.

He grunted.

"We woke you, didn't we?" She paused. "I'm sorry. I settled her as soon as I could, but everything's so dark that I had to fumble around." She paused again. "It's still snowing."

That figured. He didn't expect things to get easy all of a sudden. They were bound to get worse before they got better, and worse, at that moment, meant colder. His feet were feeling the drop in temperature in the car.

Sitting forward, he thought of the advantages of being car-bound with someone rich as he reached for the fur coat and wrapped it around his lower half.

"My boots got wet when I went outside," Lily said quietly. "They're still damp. I wasn't sure whether I'd have been warmer if I'd taken them off. You left yours on, so I figured I'd do the same."

"Are you cold?"

"I'm okay."

"What does that mean?"

"It means that I'd be a lot more comfortable if we could build a fire in here, but that I don't think I'm on the verge of frostbite yet."

"How's the baby?"

"She's all bundled up. It's a miracle I can find her under the hat and hood and snowsuit. I've kept her inside my coat, like you told me to. She's still pretty warm."

Quist looked at his wristwatch, then burrowed more deeply into his coat.

"What time is it?" Lily asked.

"Almost ten."

She moaned. "I feel like I've been sitting here forever. I was sure it had to be at least one or two in the morning."

"Time flies when you're having fun."

His sarcasm went right by her. "I want morning to come. I don't like the dark."

"Did you sleep?"

"Uh-uh. I'm too nervous." She'd spent the time since he'd fallen asleep imagining any number of possible scenarios for the next twenty-four hours. Most of them were depressing.

"Are you hungry?"

"Starved. I was waiting for you to wake up to eat."

That brought Quist slowly around. "You have food?"

"Leftovers from lunch. There's a bag on the floor on my side. Can you reach it?" She would have done it herself if Nicki hadn't been so comfortable, attached to her breast.

When he leaned over to feel around on the floor, the side of his head touched her thigh. Though she was covered not only by jeans, but by the afghan and her coat, she still felt a moment's awkwardness, which was probably why she began to talk more quickly.

"There was a Burger King on the highway. I stopped there to use the rest room and change Nicki, and I figured that I had to get something, even though I wasn't very hungry." When he straightened with the bag in his hand, she felt a little less crowded. "I don't think there's more than half a hamburger, a few fries and some cookies, and they're probably rock hard by now, but they're better than the rest of the food this airline's serving."

Quist snickered.

"If you don't mind my germs" she added.

Germs were the least of his worries. Removing the contents of the bag, he laid them out on the empty baby carrier.

Lily eyed the dim shapes. "I suppose it's lucky we can't see. We might think twice about eating."

"Not much chance of that," he said, but he made no move to take any of the food.

"I'm sorry there isn't more. I should have ordered a whole lot, but I never dreamed dinner would be a problem."

Neither had Quist, and as he stared at the meager spread, he couldn't help but wonder how many dinners in the future would be a problem. Reaching to the floor on his own side this time, he tugged out his duffel, opened it and rummaged around inside. He set down several foil cubes beside the Burger King remains, rummaged again and came up with several more.

Lily couldn't make out details in the dark. "What are they?"

"Chunky bars."

"Chunky bars?" Her voice rose. "I haven't had a Chunky in years!"

"Don't get excited. We'll have to ration them, too. It may be a while before we get our hands on anything more."

"Ration. Right."

"It's a sensible thing to do, isn't it?"

"Sure. Ooops—okay, Nicki," she said softly as she lifted the infant to her shoulder. She put her mouth to the baby's cheek and began to pat her back, breathing, "That's my girl. What an angel you are. Got a bubble in there for me?" Stopping her patting for a minute, she groped in the diaper bag, which was jammed between her leg and the side of the car. Coming up with a cloth diaper, she slid it between the baby and her shoulder. "Just in case," she murmured under her breath and started patting again.

"In case what?" Quist asked.

"In case she cheeses on my shoulder. It smells vile."

"Oh. Great. By all means, then, take the precaution. The last thing we need in here is something that smells vile."

Lily bit her lower lip, wondering what he was going to do when she changed certain diapers. In that respect she was grateful Nicki was so young. Even the worst smells weren't all that bad. Of course, that was easy for Lily to say. Nicki was flesh of her flesh.

Nuzzling the infant's cheek, she found pleasure in the sweet baby scent that lingered even now from her morning bath. How long ago that seemed, a world away. That sweet scent would disappear, she knew, if they didn't somehow get help. Thought of Nicki going without a warm bath, without lotion and powder and clean clothes disturbed her. Oh, she had the lotion and powder and clean clothes with her, but there was no way she was going to undress the infant for other than the quickest diaper change. It was too cold.

Quist interrupted her grim musings. "The only thing here with protein is the hamburg. I think you should have half now and save the rest for tomorrow."

"Me? What about you? Don't you want some?"

"I can do with the other stuff."

"But you said it yourself—this is the only thing with protein. There's none in the other stuff."

"You need it more. You're the one who's eating for two."

"That was when I was pregnant. Nicki eats for herself now."

"What—hamburg? French fries?"

"Uh, not quite."

"Exactly," he said, annoyed that she was making him spell it out. "She drinks milk. Does she eat anything solid yet?"

"No."

"So milk is it, and you're the only milkman around here, which means you need that protein more than I do."

"But you're the one who's going out in the snow tomorrow looking for help."

"I'll be fine."

"You may be walking for miles."

"I'm in shape."

"To go through a blizzard?"

"I'm not going through a blizzard. I'm not budging unless the snow stops."

"What if it doesn't" Lily asked. She tried to keep her voice steady, though it was higher than before. "What if it keeps on for two or three days—or more? What if four or five feet pile up out there? I've read of that happening in the North, and we're pretty far north. What if—"

Nicki burped. Lily held the breath she'd been about to expel, then released it slowly.

"It won't do either of us any good to worry about *what ifs*," Quist said, using an assured voice in the hope of calming her. "The fact is that for now, we're okay. We have shelter and a little food. We'll make that last as long as possible and then worry. One thing at a time. Okay?"

Lily wished she could see his face, but it was too dark, so she had to put her faith in the low command of his voice. "Okay," she whispered, then added, "I'm sorry. I try to be strong, but it doesn't work sometimes."

Her whisper, and the words she said, did strange things to Quist. Something stirred inside him, something like compassion. It was totally uncharacteristic and entirely unwanted, but he felt a definite softening. He guessed it was her honesty. At least he thought it was honesty. It had been so long since he'd connected honesty with a woman that he wasn't quite sure whether to buy it or not.

"Take the hamburg," he insisted crossly and thrust it in her direction.

"Let me finish with Nicki first."

"I thought you were starved."

"I am, but another fifteen minutes won't hurt."

"Can't you eat and nurse at the same time?"

"Yes, but then I'd be diluting each of the pleasures."

He put the hamburg down again and drawled, "And you're a lady who likes her pleasures."

Vaguely stung by his sarcasm, Lily said, "Certain ones more than others. Nursing Nicki is the best. It's the most rewarding experience I've ever had in my life, and the most innocent pleasure in the world. It's a time when there's just the two of us, and we're both doing what we were made to do. While I'm nursing, I like to give her my undivided attention. So why should I eat? It's not like I have a whole list of things to do when she's done."

That said, she transferred Nicki to her other arm, tucked her inside her coat and began the second half of the feeding.

Quist took several of the fries, slouched back into his side of the car and began to eat them slowly, one by one.

"And anyway," Lily's voice came through the darkness after several minutes, "there haven't been as many pleasures in my life as you think. I've earned everything I have."

"You work?"

"Every woman works."

He grunted. "In some form or another." He was thinking of Belinda McClean and the horizontality of her occupation. Not that he was a hypocrite. He'd enjoyed Belinda plenty and had paid her well. Then she'd gotten greedy and had blown the arrangement to bits. But that had been years ago. Ancient history.

Lily coupled his muttered comment with something else he'd said. "You don't like women, do you?"

"I don't trust women. They're only out for themselves."

"I could say the same about men."

"Then you've just met the wrong ones."

"Maybe. And maybe the same is true with you and women."

"I doubt it. In forty years, I've seen lots of women come and go, and not one of them's been able to change my mind."

Given the iron beneath his words, Lily had no doubt that he fully believed what he said. "That's very sad."

"No, it's very smart. I know what to expect and what not to. I go through life with my eyes wide open. Wide open." Having issued what he felt to be an adequate warning, he fell silent. But something was nagging at him. After several minutes, he gave in to that nagging. "So what *do* you do to get paid so well?"

"I never said I was paid well. I said I've earned everything I have."

"Did you earn the car? The clothes?" He'd seen quite a few of those clothes when they'd been taking things from the trunk, and everything he'd touched had been top-notch.

"Every last piece," she said with conviction.

"How?"

"By making a warm, welcoming home for a man who took every possible opportunity to put me down. By cooking for him, only to be told that the meat was tough—and cleaning for him, only to be told that the professional service did it better—and dressing up for him, only to be told that the particular color I'd worn made me look sick. By being there when he needed me, then having to stand by and watch when he decided he needed someone else." She caught a quick breath. "He was never particularly generous. Maybe he was just distrustful, like you. Maybe he felt that I was out to take him for whatever I could get, so that made him cautious. But what he gave me, I earned. So help me, I did."

Her voice hung in the silence of the car for a minute, then dropped, leaving nothing but the sounds of the storm to fill the void. Listening to the elements' anger, she was drained of her own. After several minutes she breathed out a small, rueful laugh.

"So much for giving Nicki my undivided attention." She pressed a gentle kiss on the infant's forehead, and said in a soft breath, "Forgive me, Nicki? I think it's the darkness that brings out the demons. Either that, or I just need to hear the sound of someone's voice, even if it's my own. I'll be better from now on. I promise I will."

True to her word, she spent the rest of the feeding doing all the little things, some vocal, some not, that told Nicki how much she was loved. And through it all, Quist sat and listened. There was more he wanted to ask, but he couldn't get himself to interrupt. Strangely, though he'd felt uncomfortable earlier, he suddenly wanted to turn on the overhead light for a minute. He wanted to see the lady beside him. She was taking on a personality, shaped by voice and words, but there was an unreality to it in the darkness.

He waited until she'd put the baby to her shoulder again. Then he asked, "How old are you?"

The question surprised her. She hadn't thought he'd care one way or another how old she was. But she had no big secrets on that score. "Twenty-nine."

In turn, that surprised him. He'd have guessed she was younger. "How long were you married?"

"Four years."

"And he just walked off with someone else and left you with a newborn child?"

"Oh, no. He left me the day I told him I was pregnant. He said I'd plotted it just to keep him." She pressed her cheek to the baby's and whispered, "As though I hadn't wanted you all along. I'd been trying all that time to get pregnant and he knew it." She spoke up again for Quist. "He thought I knew he'd been fooling around, the jackass. I wouldn't have put up with that." Her voice fell, though this time not for the baby's sake. She'd thought long and hard about what might have been, and each time she had doubts. "Then again, maybe I would have. If he'd said that his thing with Hillary was a mistake and that it was over, I might have stayed. I'm not sure I would have been able to believe him, but I did want the marriage to work."

"Why?"

That was harder to answer, because it went beyond self-doubt. Lily knew what her weaknesses were, and she wasn't proud of them. Not even cover of darkness—or the fact that Quist was a stranger—made it easy to confess. "Oh, lots of reasons," she murmured, but said no more.

He let it go, mainly because he didn't feel he had a right to pry further. The reasons why she'd wanted her marriage to work had no bearing on their present predicament. As to that predicament, all he needed from her was a little cooperation, and he felt sure he'd get that. What they *both* needed was a little luck.

Finishing off the last of the few fries he'd allotted himself, he listened to the wind and wondered about his luck. Actually he'd had his share. He had the ranch, which he'd won in a card game twenty-one years before. He'd been nineteen and brash as all get-out then, and though he hadn't known what in the hell to do with two hundred acres of land, three ramshackle buildings, a small herd of cattle and two aging cowhands, he'd known enough to take advantage of the windfall. Working his tail off and learning as he worked, he turned the ranch around, eventually adding to the acreage, the buildings, the herd and the crew. Sure, hard work had been most of it, but he'd had certain breaks, too. He'd lucked out more than once when it came to contacts and timing and deals, health and weather.

He sure as hell hadn't lucked out with women, though.

"I take it you're not married," Lily said. Much as she tried, she couldn't put the discussion to rest.

"You take right."

"Have you ever thought about being married?"

"Nope. Never even came close."

"I mean, have you ever imagined yourself being married and thought about what it would be like?"

"No."

"Never thought about how you'd handle it, how you'd react to some things as a husband?"

"Never."

Since she wasn't getting the answers she wanted, she turned her attention to Nicki. "Where's that bubble?" she whispered gently. She brushed her lips across the infant's forehead, then ran a thumb over her cheek and would have repeated the gesture if her hands hadn't been so cold. Tugging the sleeves of her jacket over them, she began rubbing firm, flat-handed circles over the baby's back. Several rounds of that brought a soft burp from the small bundle. Lavishing whispered praise, she righted her clothes and returned the baby to the crook of her elbow.

Quist propped a foot on the gear shift. "Why do you ask?"

"Ask what?"

"About marriage." There had been three questions, one right after the next, all about the same thing. He wanted to know why.

"Oh, I was just wondering about something, but if you've never imagined what married life would be like, there's no point in my asking."

"Ask."

"No. I think not."

"Why?"

"Because you don't like women, so I know just what you'll say."

"That's one of the things I like *least* about women. They think they know it all." He raised his voice. "You don't know me. How can you know what I'll say?"

Annoyed that he was making something out of nothing, she burst back, "All I wanted to know was whether you thought Jarrod was right. If you got married, if you took vows and promised to be faithful, would you turn around and cheat on your wife? Do all men do it? Is there some justification for it that I'm missing? I mean, I took those vows seriously. Am I the one marching to a different drummer? Is that my problem? Am I misinterpreting the rules of the game?"

Quist didn't know what to say. She was clearly hurt, but he was no healer.

"And it wasn't only Jarrod," she went on, as though once started she couldn't hold it in. "It was loads of guys we knew. I always heard women talk about this one or that one who was fooling around. No one ever named Jarrod in front of me, and I was never sure whether to believe them about the others until Jarrod told me, and even *then* I might have thought he was exaggerating, trying to okay what he'd done by claiming all the guys were doing it, until Michael came on to me. *Michael.* Jarrod's own *brother—*"

Only after she'd said it did she realize what she'd done. Breathing hard, she buried her face by Nicki's until she'd regained a bit of control. Then she raised her head enough to be able to speak clearly—softly, but clearly.

"I'm sorry. I got carried away. It's history—water over the dam. There isn't a lot I can do about what happened. But it still hurts. I guess I'm still pretty angry."

Quist could believe that. But he wasn't about to pass judgment, to say whether or not she had a right to that anger, because he'd only heard one side of the story. For all he knew, the innocent-sounding little mother huddled close by had been a shrew of a wife. For all he knew, she was a lousy lover, or, conversely, a pathological liar who hadn't taken her marriage vows half as seriously as she'd like him to believe. For all he knew, she'd been feeding him a line of bull.

He didn't think so, but what the hell, he didn't even know her name. It was, he realized, time to change that.

"Who are you?"

"Excuse me?"

"Your name—you never told me what it was."

She was silent for a minute. He was starting to think that she did indeed have something to hide, when she laughed. It was a soft, self-conscious sound. "I don't believe it. I just dumped all the sordid little details of my marriage in your lap, and you don't even know my name."

"Well?"

"Lily. Lily Danziger."

"Is Danziger your—"

"Maiden name. Nicki's birth certificate reads Danziger, too." Her voice hardened. "Jarrod didn't want any part of us, and the feeling's mutual."

"What about child support?"

"What about it?"

"Don't you want any money?"

"No."

"Don't you *need* any money? I hear raising a kid is expensive these days."

"It's always been expensive, but people manage."

"How will you? Do you have money of your own?"

"I'm not independently wealthy, no."

"Then you must've got a great divorce settlement."

"Why do you say that?"

"Because it makes sense," he said, and because he was naturally cynical when it came to women. "The guy you married has money—he leaves you for another woman the day you tell him you're pregnant—you go through the pregnancy all by yourself and give birth to the child alone. I mean, it's a tear-jerker."

"I don't hear you crying."

He snorted. "I'm not."

"You're just a hard-as-nails kind of guy."

His voice took on the hard-as-nails sound she'd heard so much of at the start. "I'm a survivor. I do what I have to do, say what I have to say, feel what I have to feel."

"And you're out for number one, just like Jarrod."

"Lady, if I was out for number one, I wouldn't have offered to share my Chunky bars with you."

"It's Lily, not lady," she huffed, "and you can keep your damned Chunky bars. I wouldn't eat them, anyway."

"Why not?" he asked, vaguely affronted.

"Because if I eat chocolate while I'm nursing, the baby is apt to get diarrhea."

"Oh."

"Yes, oh." With that, she turned her back on him, making herself as comfortable as possible with Nicki safely tucked inside her coat. She didn't want to talk to Quist anymore. He annoyed her. So she half sat, half lay on her side of the car with her hooded head pressed to the wool slacks she'd used to line the window.

The wind blew. She tried not to hear it, tried not to hear the hard nuggets of snow that swirled with it, hitting small bared patches of the car. She tried not to think about the cold that had settled in her hands and feet and threatened to spread, and she tried not to think about the future. Mostly she tried not to cry, which was what she really wanted to do. She'd been wanting to do it a lot lately, and it had nothing to do with a snowstorm. It had to do with facing a future that was unknown and daunting. It had to do with feeling very alone and very frightened.

Quist, too, listened to the storm, but his eyes were on her huddled form, trying to make sense of it in the darkness. He didn't know why he bothered, didn't know why he didn't just turn over and go back to sleep. He was still exhausted, but he wasn't as cold as he figured she was, and that made him feel bad.

She seemed so damned fragile. He wanted to think her irresponsible when it came to driving, lousy when it came to keeping a husband and greedy when it came to getting rid of one—still, she seemed fragile. And if there was one thing he had to hand her, she seemed like a devoted mother.

Which was a hell of a lot more than his own had been, he mused, then broke into his musings when he heard a strange sound. It wasn't the baby, at least he didn't think it was.

He held his breath for a minute and listened, then cautiously said, "Lily?"

There was a pause, then a muted, "Mmm?"

He waited, trying to hear the sound again, but it didn't come. "Are you all right?"

After another pause, she said, "I'm fine."

Sitting up, he reached forward and switched on the overhead light.

Lily's head came around fast. She didn't have to squint; the light was too small for that. But it wasn't small enough to hide the tears that pooled on her lower lids—or the defiance behind those tears.

"Don't you dare say a word," she warned, eyes glittering. "Don't you dare tell me that I'm weak or that there's something wrong with me—because I'm tired of hearing it."

He hadn't been about to say either of those things. He'd been about to swear, because tears usually meant that a woman wanted something, and he didn't have a damn thing to give just then. But he decided that swearing wasn't such a good idea, either. It would only upset her, and he didn't want her upset. It wouldn't help the situation.

"I just wanted to make sure you eat," he said. He picked up the half hamburger and held it out. "Like I said, you're the only one who can feed the kid."

The sight of the cold sandwich reminded Lily of how hungry she was. "Can you tear it in half?" she asked. When he'd done it, she took one of the two pieces. "Are you sure you won't have the other?"

"I'm sure."

"If you want it later, you can have it."

But he shook his head. He felt guilty enough about eating the few fries he had, since she wouldn't share his candy. So what was hers was hers. He'd still give her a Chunky if she changed her mind—and it might come to that if the choice were between some milk and no milk—but he wasn't taking any more of her food. She needed it.

Setting the uneaten quarter hamburger on the carrier with the rest of the food, he turned off the light again and sat back. He could feel Lily beside him, eating slowly. He couldn't hear whether her breathing was even—the wind made that hard—but at least he didn't hear another gasp or swallow or whatever the hell it had been. He didn't want her crying. He didn't like women at all, but women who cried were the worst.

On that thought he closed his eyes, slid lower on the seat and went to sleep.

When he awoke, it was six-thirty in the morning, dawn was just beginning to break and Lily was feeding the baby. He wasn't at all where he wanted to be, which put him instantly on his guard and made him cross. He would have complained that the infant's cries had woken him if it were true. But he couldn't remember hearing the baby. He'd been exhausted. Though he'd gone with little sleep many a time back home, the sheer frustration of this trip had taken the toll that physical strain rarely did.

Now there was physical strain, too. Gingerly he stretched muscles that were stiff from the unnatural position he'd slept in and from the cold.

Feeling his movement, Lily peered around the hood of her parka. She was relieved that he'd awakened to face the day with her, but Jarrod's dark early-morning moods had conditioned her to caution.

Quist had never awoken to a woman's stare before. "Something wrong?" he demanded in an edgy voice.

"No."

"Why are you looking at me that way?"

Quickly she looked away, toward where Nicki was nursing under the afghan. "No reason." She took a fast breath. "The wind is down, but I can't tell if the snow has stopped. Everything's quiet. That has to be a good sign, doesn't it?"

Quist flexed his shoulder. "Snow doesn't make much noise when it falls on itself." He studied her downcast face. Even in profile, even in the dim light of dawn, he saw signs of strain. "Did you sleep?"

"I dozed. I kept thinking . . . lousy things."

He didn't want to hear what those lousy things were.

But she couldn't help herself. The night had been so long, hour after hour with only the briefest of catnaps, and during those waking times her imagination had been in full swing. Now that there was someone to talk to, she needed reassurance. "I kept thinking that maybe there'd be so much snow piled up around the car that we wouldn't be able to open the door."

"We'll be able to open the door."

"I kept thinking that maybe it would freeze shut, and that we wouldn't have any way of melting the ice, so we'd be stuck in here, *really* stuck in here." She swallowed and whispered, "That won't happen, will it?"

"No." The question, he knew, was whether there was anything outside that could offer them better shelter than the car. Sitting forward to stretch the cramped muscles of his back, he glanced around toward the general vicinity where the baby would be under the afghan. "Is she all right?"

Lily nodded. "She slept, thank goodness, and she's drinking well. I don't look forward to changing her. She's so small, and it's so cold. Her legs tremble pathetically. But if I don't change her, she'll be uncomfortable that way, and if she gets diaper rash, it'll be worse." She fell silent for a minute, then raised her eyes to Quist and said in a small voice, "When I'm not thinking about being frozen solid in this car, I'm thinking of being rescued. Do you think it will happen?"

"Nope," was Quist's blunt reply. "No one's going to find us here. It's up to us to find someone or something out there." He reached for one of the Chunky bars, peeled back the foil covering, snapped the bar in half and popped one of the halves into his mouth. Rewrapping the other half, he put it back with the rest of their meager store of food. Then he crawled into the front seat, jammed the Stetson onto his head and forced the door open. He was out, with the door slammed shut behind him, before Lily could tell whether the swirling snow was simply snow dislodged from the car or a continuation of the storm.

The minutes crept by, and with each, Lily grew more apprehensive. She had no idea whether Quist was gone for the day, gone for good, or simply looking around outside. As had happened the evening before when he'd left the car, she felt an overwhelming aloneness. At least it was getting lighter out, but that was small solace if, in fact, he'd set off on his own.

When the door opened, she felt an inordinate sense of relief. Her gaze clung to his snowy figure as he slid back into the car. Nervously she awaited his verdict.

Hauling his duffel from under the seat, he began rummaging inside. "It's stopped snowing for now, but there's more to come. The sky's still filled with it. I'm going to see how far I can get before that happens." Shrugging out of his heavy sheepskin jacket, he pulled a sweater on over the one he was already wearing.

Lily's eyes clung to his shoulders. Their breadth represented the strength she'd soon be losing. "Which direction are you going in?"

"Ahead." He pulled on the jacket. "Behind is a waste. You didn't see anything there yesterday. There won't be anything there today." Reaching into the bag, he pulled out several pairs of socks. "Besides, it's all uphill, and I don't have snowshoes. Better to hike down. I'll go for three or four hours or until the road comes to an end. With luck I'll hit something before then." He stuffed a pair of socks in each of his pockets, took a third pair in his hand and looked her in the eye. "It may be a while before I get back."

"How much of a while?" she asked, unable to hide her fear.

"That depends on what I find. But I don't want you to leave the car. Do you understand that? If you start wandering around, you'll get lost."

"What about you? What if you get lost?"

"I won't. I'm a tracker." His eyes sharpened. "But it won't do me any good to go out searching for help and come back and find you gone. Stay right here with the baby. I don't care how impatient you get, do not wander away from this car.

If you start stumbling around in the snow, you'll be in trouble. Do you understand what I'm saying?"

He was speaking in such a slow, clear, elementary kind of way that she couldn't help but understand. "I'm not dumb."

"But you're scared, and scared women do crazy things. So I'm telling you—stay here, stay as warm as you can and remember to eat. Sooner or later, I'll be back."

"Sooner or later?" she echoed in a small voice.

"I can't tell when it will be."

"Will it be today?"

"With luck."

"And if it's not?"

"If it's not, you'll spend another night like the one you've just spent, and I'll be back tomorrow."

"Will you?"

"Yes."

"Do you promise?"

Quist wasn't used to having his word questioned. He wouldn't have put up with it, if Lily hadn't looked so damned frightened. And vulnerable. Damn, he didn't need vulnerable. "I just said it, didn't I?"

She nodded. "But can I believe you?"

He studied her closely. "You're not a very trusting sort."

"I've trusted and been hurt."

That much was clear from the factual way she said it and the sober look in her eye. It also jibed with things she'd told him about herself. Feeling an empathy he didn't want, Quist drew himself up as straight as he could within the confines of the car. "Then you've trusted the wrong men. Me, I'm a man of my word. If I say I'll be back, I'll be back."

Looking into the coal-black eyes that told her nothing in the dim light of dawn, Lily wavered for a minute. Then she thought back on the past fourteen hours and realized that though Quist had his moods, he'd behaved responsibly. She also realized that she had no choice; if she was to make it through his absence with her peace of mind intact, she had to believe that he'd be back.

"Okay?" he asked in a low, cautious tone.

She nodded, then watched him tuck the half of the Chunky bar he hadn't eaten into his pocket.

"In case I get hungry," he explained, then snorted and added, "as if I couldn't eat ten of them now." His dark eyes met hers. "So you've got the rest of the food. I'll have to come back to get it, won't I?"

Before she had time to respond, he let himself out and slammed the door.

3

FOR QUIST, the trudge through the snow was cold and frustrating. He followed the narrow break in the trees on the assumption that it was a road, though eighteen inches of snow had obliterated any sure signs. Save for that lean swath, the landscape was reduced to an endless expanse of snow-laden woods. A winter wonderland? More like the twilight zone, he knew. Oh, he was hardy enough. He could survive cold and lack of food; he'd done it before and he'd do it again.

The problem was Lily. He figured she'd be able to make it through another couple of nights in the car, but after that there'd be trouble. She was cold, and unless he got something to eat, her milk would dry up, and if that happened, the baby would starve, and if *that* happened—he didn't want to even think about it. God only knew why he cared; Lily Danziger and her baby were nothing to him but a pain in the butt. Still, he couldn't just let them freeze.

The more he thought about it—and he had little else to think about as he trudged on through the snow—it was incredible. From the cradle on, he'd had no need for a woman, yet he'd been involved with his share, and each one had been trouble. Hell, he would never have been in the goddamned Maine woods in the first place if it hadn't been for a woman, and now another's plight had him stomping his way for help.

Sure, he'd be stomping his way for help even if he'd been the only one stuck. He wasn't about to freeze to death, either. But the fact was that if he'd been alone, he'd never have left the main road in the first place. And if he were alone, he wouldn't feel the responsibility he did now.

He knew what he wanted. He wanted to hit a bona fide thoroughfare, flag down a car, find a can of gas and some chains to get Lily's fancy red Audi out of the snow. He wasn't even sure if chains would do the trick, especially if it started to snow again. Playing it safe, he'd probably snag a tow truck to go in after her. If all went well, he'd be in his own motel room for the night, then back on his way to Quebec in the morning.

If all went well.

Somehow he didn't think it would. After plodding through the snow for nearly two hours, he saw no sign of civilization. There wasn't the faintest smell of a wood fire. There wasn't the slightest sound of a snow plow. Maine was nowhere near as big as Montana, and the terrain wasn't nearly as rugged, still he felt well and truly isolated from humanity. In Montana that was good. In Maine, he wasn't so sure.

FOR LILY, the wait was interminable. With the full dawning of day, she stepped out of the car into knee-deep snow, which did nothing to reassure her. Even if she had gas, she doubted the Audi would be able to make it back to the main road. True, it had stopped snowing, but the sky was still that pregnant, pale gray shade it had been the day before. Quist was right. The snow wasn't done.

Back in the car, she piled every imaginable layer over her for warmth, then played with Nicki, who was right with her under all the covers. She sang; she cooed and babbled and hummed. She took advantage of daylight to do all the things she wouldn't be able to do once night fell again, though she prayed something would happen before then. She wasn't a camper. A city person born and bred, she'd never spent time in the country. As hard as it was to believe that she'd already spent one cold night in the car, it was that much harder to believe that there might be more nights like it.

She wondered how long she'd be able to survive that way, then decided not to think about it. But minutes later she was wondering what would happen if Quist was lost or hurt in the snow and never made it to civilization. Her car, she realized, could be sitting just where it was, unseen by human eyes until spring came, if then.

She wouldn't let that happen. If Quist didn't return in a day or two, she knew that despite what he'd told her, she'd set out on her own. She wasn't about to let Nicki die. She wasn't about to die, herself. She had something to prove, something to do with basic human worth, and she was damned if she'd let a snowstorm and a few wrong turns stand in her way.

Still, her empty stomach knotted. She listened for the sound of a rescuing tow truck, but none came. She waited for Quist to return with the news that he'd found a settlement several hills over, in which case they could laugh at the night they'd spent thinking themselves marooned. But he didn't come.

One hour passed, then two, then three. Nicki slept for a bit and awoke hungry. After Lily fed her, she finished off the last of the cold hamburger. An hour later she had a cookie, but by then she realized the importance of saving whatever she had. Quist had been gone for four hours. Clearly he hadn't found something nearby. Things didn't look good.

Noontime came and went. She rocked Nicki, sang playful songs to her, though playfulness was the last thing she felt. At one point tears came to her eyes and, holding Nicki tight, she cried quietly. She felt she had that right. With the exception of Nicki's arrival, the past year had been a nightmare, and the nightmare went on, more vivid, if anything, in the week now past. From Michael's attack, to her precipitous departure from Hartford, to the long drive, the snowstorm and now this—she feared to think of where it would end.

If her parents were alive, she'd have had a haven, humble as it was. But her mother had been dead for ten years, her father for four, and she had no siblings to ask for help. All she wanted, she realized, was to feel a little less alone.

Sitting in her car, snowbound and lost in the middle of God's country, did nothing to ease that feeling of aloneness. Nor did Quist's continuing absence. By the time one o'clock came, he'd been gone for nearly six hours. She told herself that he'd reached help, but that it would take time for that help to get back to her. Still she felt abandoned—and colder and more frightened by the minute.

At one-forty, just when she was beginning to despair, there was a sudden wrench on the door. It opened with a yawn and a snow-covered figure fell inside.

Had it not been for the Stetson, Lily wasn't sure she'd have recognized him, but the Stetson came quickly off, as did the socks that had been tied end-to-end to cover his ears and the large sheepskin jacket, and before she knew what was happening, he was in the back seat with her, crawling into the nest that her body heat had managed to keep warmer than the air.

"Damn, it's cold out there," he said hoarsely. He pulled her close, baby and all.

"You're freezing!" she cried. She was shocked not only by the chill of his body but by the sudden intimacy he'd forced on her. Much as she told herself that the circumstances were extenuating, it had been a long time since she'd been so close to a man.

"I know. Warm me a little before we go back out?"

Her shock yielded to a glimmer of hope. "You found something?"

"A cabin. It's a one-room job, but it's been lived in as recently as last summer." He took a shivering breath against her forehead. "There's a woodstove, plenty of wood and some food—canned goods and staples. I would've lit the stove if I hadn't been afraid to leave it untended. Didn't want to get you and the kid there and find the place burned down." He paused. "It's a three-hour walk. Can you make it?"

"I can make it."

"You just had a baby. Are you sure?"

"It's been five weeks."

"Still, you must be—your body can't be right yet."

"It's okay. I can make it."

He figured he had to take her word for it. "Fine, then. Strap the kid close to your body and wear as many layers of clothes as possible. We'll carry whatever else we can. God knows how long we'll be there."

Lily started to get up, but he snagged her back with an arm around her waist.

"In a minute," he murmured, his voice a deep rumble against her temple while his legs tangled with hers. "Just a minute. You're the only thing warm worth a damn for miles, and I'm cold. Give me another minute. You owe me that much."

He was right, she knew. He'd found a place that would keep them alive, and he could easily have stayed there to warm up, eat and relax for a while, but he'd turned right around and come back to her. That had to say something for his character.

Not that his body was all that bad, either. With the passing of her initial shock, she realized that the closeness felt good. She guessed it had something to do with the hours she'd just spent alone and fearing the worst. She half suspected she'd have welcomed the closeness of a baboon. But Quist was no baboon. He smelled of the cold outdoors, of snow and of man in a pleasant sort of way. Though he burrowed close, she didn't feel stifled, and beneath the surface chill of his body was a certain strength.

She could have done worse, far worse than this cowboy, she knew, and yes, she owed him.

Maintaining a safe grip on Nicki, she slipped her free arm around his head to cover his ears, which, in spite of the thick hair that brushed them and the makeshift earmuffs he'd worn, were red from the cold.

Quist wasn't about to reject the gesture. He welcomed anything of a warming nature after the trek he'd made, and the trek wasn't over. They had to make it back to the cabin by nightfall, which wouldn't be a problem if he was alone, but he doubted Lily could match his pace. The snow on the ground was deep, and new snow had begun falling a short time before. The additional inches wouldn't make things any easier.

He supposed that the sooner they set out, the better. But he didn't move. It felt too good to lie there absorbing the warmth of a woman, even if she was a scrawny thing—with a bawling kid.

"What's wrong with her?"

"I think she's being squished," Lily said and loosened the arm she'd wrapped around Quist's head. It was a minute before she extricated herself enough to push up against the seat, another minute before she'd worked through the layers to reach the baby's face. "What is it, pumpkin?" she whispered. "Shh. It's all right. Shh."

Nicki kept crying, her tiny features pinched and pink.

"Is she hungry?" Quist asked, sitting up beside them.

"She shouldn't be. Not for another hour."

"Can you put her down while we get ready to go?"

"She'll cry, but that's okay." She paused. "If you can take it." Expectantly she looked up into his face. It was closer than she'd thought, and though he wore a day's worth of stubble and a frown, she wasn't frightened.

Intrigued was more like it. Tanned from the sun and ruddy from the cold, he was the image of health. With his shadowed jaw, the squint marks by his eyes and the general set of his features, he was also the image of ruggedness. Not bad looking, she had to admit. Something like the Marlboro man.

She'd never met a Marlboro man before. Ruggedness wasn't something a man developed at Harvard Law, or Columbia Law, or Yale Law, and since she'd worked in posh law offices for years, most of the men she'd known had gone to one of the three. That meant they'd graduated with credentials to match their egos—largely overrated, in her modest opinion.

Ruggedness, on the other hand, was hard earned. In that sense, Quist was refreshing. He was also looking into her eyes in a way that was every bit as cock-sure as any one of the high-powered lawyers she'd known.

"I can take it," he said. "We'll stuff my duffel and one of your bags. And that diaper thing over there. And anything else that can be strung over a shoulder. Right before we leave, feed her, change her, do whatever else you have to to keep her happy while we hike. You won't be feeding her again until we reach the cabin."

Lily agreed that the plan made sense. "Is the cabin on the main road?"

"Main road?" he asked in a mocking tone that brought back yesterday's folly.

Lily figured she owed him that, too. "This road," she conceded without a fight. "Will we have any trouble finding it?"

"I'm a tracker. I told you that. I don't get lost." He didn't tell her that he'd had to try several different forks in the road before he'd found one that led to a cabin, because it didn't matter. He had found the cabin. And he could find it again. Enough said.

Lily studied his face for a minute longer, then took a deep, resigned, if faintly unsteady breath. "You came back for me when you didn't have to. I suppose I can trust you not to lead me out into the snow for nothing."

The element of resignation struck Quist the wrong way. He bristled. "It's my life, too, lady. Just remember that."

"Lily. It's Lily, not lady."

He put his face even closer. "Warm me up, and it's Lily. Talk snotty, and it's lady."

"I didn't talk—"

"You sounded all stuck-up and put out."

"I didn't—"

"You're the one who got us into this mess, remember?"

"I thought—"

"You thought wrong. Fancy city girl screws up again, only this time the stakes are higher than usual. Face it, sweetheart, you need me."

"I am not your sweetheart."

His eyes flashed hotly. "And ain't it a shame. You'll never know that particular pleasure, will you?" Leaving Lily tongue-tied, he bolted forward, tugged on his coat, hat and makeshift earmuffs, then stomped out of the car to get a bag from the trunk.

Lily spent a minute getting over her astonishment, then another trying to figure out what had happened. Snotty...stuck-up...put out...she hadn't felt any of those things. She thought she'd been telling him she trusted him. It should have been a compliment. Obviously he hadn't taken it that way. He certainly did expect the worst where women were concerned.

But he expected other things, too. That last look in his eyes told her so. It had been different. Hot and flashing. Challenging in a sexual kind of way. No doubt he'd been thinking of one of the women he loved to hate.

A dull thud from the trunk brought her around. Reluctant to give Quist cause for further complaint, she gave the still-crying Nicki a quick hug. "Hush, Nicki. I have to put you down for a couple of minutes. Please don't cry. Please." When the crying momentarily lessened, she set the infant in the car seat and quickly went out after Quist.

It didn't take them long to select the most malleable of Lily's canvas bags and empty it of all but practical items. Returning to the car, they repacked it with the heavier clothing that they'd brought in the evening before. When that was done, they stuffed Quist's duffel and the baby's bag with more of the same, sliding diapers into every imaginable crevice.

They worked in silence. As though to compensate, Nicki kept up a stream of sound that varied from faint whimpering to all-out rage. Finally Lily picked her up and changed her, then put her to her breast. Only then was she still. And only then, with that brief idle time to pass until they left, did Quist pull a can from his pocket. Using one of the arms of his pocket knife, he opened the can, and using a flat blade, scooped out a helping of its contents.

"Here." He held out the knife with its offering. His tone brooked no argument, and Lily gave him none. She was desperately hungry, feeling weak from it. "Carefully," he warned as she closed her mouth around the food. Gingerly she drew it into her mouth without cutting herself on the blade.

"Hash?" she asked with a curious smile. It was hard to tell with everything so cold and Quist's large hand obliterating the label on the can.

He helped himself to a mouthful, talking around the food. "Sure ain't caviar."

"It could be. It tastes heavenly. Thank you for bringing it."

"I figured it'd help before the walk."

"You figured right. My legs are a little wobbly."

He gave her another helping of the hash. "Are you sure you can make it? Better think about it before we set out."

She swallowed. "What's my alternative?"

"Staying here. Waiting for me to bring help back in."

"That's no alternative. I'm going."

"It's a long walk. If you get tired, I can't carry you."

"You won't have to," she informed him with her chin set firm. "I may have just had a baby, but I've probably had more exercise since she's been born than in the year before. I can hold my own. And Nicki. All you have to do is lead the way."

Between the look in her eye and the determination in her voice, Quist saw that she meant it. "Done," he said and knifed more hash into his mouth. He continued alternately feeding Lily, then himself, while she fed the baby beneath cover of her clothes. When she'd finished, she strapped Nicki onto her chest, pulled on several additional sweaters, her long woolen coat, then her parka, secured the fastenings as best she could, grabbed hold of the diaper bag and followed Quist out of the car.

As promised, he led the way. Carrying both his duffel and her large bag, with her fur draped over his head, he looked even more mountainous than he had when Lily had first picked him up. She had a better idea of what was inside now, though, and he wasn't the enemy.

Nature was. Snow was falling in large, moist clumps that accumulated with frightening speed on top of all that already lay on the ground. With each footstep, she sank up to her knees in the stuff, and though she walked in Quist's tracks, her boots were quickly coated.

Mercifully there was little wind, which meant that the cold wasn't exaggerated. But it was bad enough. Stealthily it crept through seams, folds and the tiniest openings that she'd thought secured. She feared to think what would have been if she were less voluminously covered. Though the layers of bulky clothing she wore made walking more difficult, they were a protection. Keeping Nicki from the chill was critical. She felt she was doing that.

The first hour passed. Quist, who had been regularly turning to check on Lily, waited for her to catch up. "Are you okay?"

She managed a stiff-jawed, "I think so."

"Need to rest?"

"No!" she insisted. "Keep going!"

With a single nod he turned and headed off again. He'd have stopped if she'd had to, but he, too, wanted to keep on. The large, moist flakes of snow had given way to smaller, colder chips that were coming down in even greater intensity. If he were to guess, he'd say that those chips were the start of an entirely new storm, which meant that the sooner he and Lily reached the cabin, the better.

By the end of the second hour, Lily was tiring badly, but again, when Quist asked if she wanted to stop for a rest, she refused. She set her sights on resting at the cabin, with a roof for shelter and a woodstove for warmth. She didn't protest, though, when he pressed one of the leftover cookies into her mouth. She needed quick energy. She needed energy, period.

On and on they plodded. Lily kept her head tucked low against the sharp nuggets that were being driven now by a rising wind. There were times when she closed her eyes and concentrated on nothing more complex than the heavy rhythm of the trek. Once when she was doing that, she plowed right into Quist, who had stopped for a minute. She nearly fell. He steadied her with a hand on either arm.

His eyes sought hers. "What's wrong?"

She wanted to tell him that she felt lousy, that her back hurt, her shoulder pinched, her insides ached, her feet were half-frozen and *where was his goddamned cabin already*. Instead, she said, "Nothing."

"How's the kid?" he asked. Thinking to lighten the mood, he quipped, "Is she still alive and kicking in there?"

It was the wrong thing to say. Lily's eyes filled up. "Of course, she's alive! I can feel her squirming. But you don't hear her screaming, do you? She's being good. So good."

Quist wasn't sure he'd be able to hear a thing through the layers Lily wore, and what small peeps might have escaped would be swallowed up by the wind. But he wasn't about to make the same mistake twice. "You're right. She's being very good. We're lucky." He paused. "Think you can make it a little longer?"

She nodded.

Some of her discouragement must have shown in her eyes because he said, "You're doin' real well, Lily. Keep it up, we're almost there," before he turned and went on.

The third hour was the tough one, as Quist knew it would be. For one thing, dusk was approaching, and though there was still enough light to see the way, night became a deadline, fast closing in. For another the terrain grew trickier closer to the cabin, and Lily's fatigue didn't help. She had trouble on the inclines, even more on the declines. He could feel the strain of those downhill stretches in his own thighs and had to believe that it would be even worse for her. At one point he turned to find that she'd stumbled and fallen in the snow, and the look on her face was so pathetic when he helped her up that he stayed by her side, rearranging the bags on his shoulders so that he could link an arm through hers to help her along.

Once she recovered from the fall, she protested his help. "I'm okay."

"You're not."

"I can manage."

"Another fall like that and you might really hurt yourself."

She'd already hurt herself, if the new discomfort in her wrist was any indication. "But I'm slowing you down."

"You'd slow me down whether I was holding your arm or not. Now keep still and walk. We're almost there."

He'd been saying that for hours, Lily thought, but she didn't have the energy to point it out. And the fact was that she did appreciate his help. Her legs seemed a great distance away, barely belonging to her, they were so cold and numb. Her gloved hands were nearly as bad, and the rest of her felt a rising chill.

Aside from the occasional stirring she'd mentioned, Nicki slept on, for which Lily was overwhelmingly grateful. She wasn't sure whether it was the steady movement that kept the infant sated or the crying she'd done that had exhausted her, but Lily couldn't begin to think of what she'd do if the baby woke and began to fuss. She couldn't very well change a diaper in the snow. Or nurse. If her milk wasn't frozen solid. Lord, what would she do if something happened to her milk?

The storm intensified as dusk deepened, and every one of Lily's fears paraded in turn through her panicked mind. While not panicked, Quist grew increasingly concerned. The cabin was ahead; he knew he hadn't taken a wrong turn, but he feared he might if they didn't reach it soon. Between the wind-whipped snow and the dark, visibility was decreasing by the minute.

"Where is it?" Lily wailed at the moment her knees buckled.

Quist caught her up. "Whoa," he said, hugging her to him for a minute, "take it easy. We're almost there. Almost there."

"I don't feel well," she cried softly.

"Just a little longer. Hang in there just a little longer."

"How much?"

"Ten, fifteen minutes, maybe."

"I don't . . . know if I can."

"Sure you can. You've come this far. A little longer's a piece of cake."

"No, it's hell."

"Then it's hell," he agreed in a harder voice, "but you've got to do it. If you can't do it for yourself, do it for Nicki. Or do it for me. I've been puttin' out for you all day. It's right time you put out for me, babe."

She was silent for a minute, and he was beginning to fear he had a *real* problem on his hands when she muttered stiffly, "It's Lily. Not babe. Lily."

"Fink out on me, and it's babe. Give me that extra go and it's anything your sweet little heart desires. So. Are we on?"

In answer, she straightened, pulled herself away and set off—unfortunately in the wrong direction, but Quist was quick to correct that, and they were soon once again huddled together, plowing through the storm.

Ten or fifteen minutes, he'd said, but Lily's concept of
time was as distorted as the landscape, an endless expanse
of snow and trees of a deepening indigo hue. She was sure
they'd been walking for another hour before they stumbled
over a rise and he tightened his grip on her arm.

"There. There it is. See it?"

She wanted to so badly, but things were blurring. "No,"
she cried feebly. Her lungs hurt. "It's too dark."

"Come on. When we're closer you'll see."

And she did, though at first she thought she was hallu-
cinating. Quist tugged her up to the door and pushed it
open, then pulled her inside and shouldered the door shut
against the havoc of the snow. Leaving her balanced against
the rough-hewn wood, he dropped the fur coat and made
his way in the dark across the small room to the table where
he'd deliberately left a hurricane lamp and a box of matches.
It took a bit of fumbling—his fingers weren't much warmer
than Lily's and he was trying to hurry—but he soon lit the
wick. The lamp cast a low glow to the room.

Lily didn't think to look around. Sliding down the door
to the floor when her legs refused to support her any longer,
she kept her eyes on Quist, who went on to light the woodstove. Dry and ready, the kindling caught, then the logs,
and the glow cast by the lamp was heightened by a warmer
one. He knelt for a minute with his hands held out to that
warmth before tossing aside his hat and earmuffs. Sitting
back on the floor directly in front of the flames, he tugged
off his boots, then stood and went at his coat. When it was
off, he looked back at Lily. She hadn't moved.

Swearing softly, he crossed to the door and knelt before
her. Small baby sounds were coming from under the layers
of her clothes. Lily heard them, but for the first time since
the baby's birth, she simply lacked the strength to move.

"I'll just . . . rest for a minute," she whispered.

"Nuh-uh. Not yet." He tugged her feet out from under her, ignoring the muffled moans the movement caused. When he'd pulled off her boots, he unfastened both her parka and the wool coat she'd worn beneath it.

"Nooo," she cried softly when he slid a hand inside and pushed the two coats away. "I'm too cold."

"The fire will warm you now." As quickly as he could, he stripped off the two oversized sweaters she'd worn. With the baby still strapped to her chest, he scooped her up, carried her the short distance to the woodstove and sat her down on the floor. "Don't move."

Why she'd have wanted to, she didn't know. He was right; the fire was warming. She couldn't quite feel it in her hands and feet, and those parts of her face that had been exposed still felt as though they belonged to someone else, but elsewhere she was beginning to feel the blessed relief of the newborn fire. If anything, though, that small thawing made her more aware of her exhaustion, which raised another point. She couldn't have moved if she'd *tried*, other than to keel over, and she didn't want to do that. The baby was crying. She had to take care of the baby.

Quist returned, dragging a mattress across the floor. With an ease that belied his own fatigue, he lifted her onto it, repositioning her directly before the flames. In the next minute he was draping an old blanket around her shoulders, and in the next, he was beside her, trying to figure out how to lift the whimpering baby from her chest.

He'd never held a baby before, and even if he knew what to grab, this one was bundled up in a snowsuit that made it difficult to see what was where. He pushed a hand between the back of the snowsuit and the canvas carrier, but there was no hold there. He reached for either arm of the snowsuit, but the baby's own arms felt so fragile through the bulky material that he was sure he'd break something if he pulled. Carefully he closed his fists on the snowsuit material alone, hoping to haul the child up that way, but the entire carrier rose with his tugs. Frustrated, he began to fiddle with the carrier itself, but the only thing contact with the side straps taught him was that though Lily's body was slender, her breasts were firm and full.

Snatching his hands away, he growled. "How in the hell does this come off?"

Lily's numbness was beginning to fade, but she'd started to shiver. It was the cold's way of exiting her body, she supposed, and in that it was good, but it did nothing to help the cause of her hands. Futilely she picked at the fastening that held the carrier close, but it was Quist who completed the job, while she cupped an arm around Nicki.

Bending forward, she deposited the baby onto the mattress, and, by a miracle of will, managed to unzip the snowsuit on the first try. She got as far as freeing the baby's tiny arms and legs from their covering when she stopped, eyes filling with tears.

She wasn't sure if it was the sight of Nicki, so relieved to be out of her snowsuit for the first time in a day and a half that she'd stopped crying and was propelling her little arms and legs in wild circles. Or if it was the simple realization that they'd made it alive through the storm. Or an accumulation of everything that had happened. But the tears trickled down her cheeks while more welled up, and she could do nothing but yield to the quiet sobs that shook her.

Staring at her, Quist felt more helpless than he ever had in his life. Oh, yeah, she was a crier, and he hated women who cried, but this one was different. Her tears were spontaneous. She wasn't turning them on for his sake, because he doubted she was aware of his existence just then. She was crying because she'd gone through a hell of a lot in the last day and she needed the outlet.

He wasn't sure he could complain. She'd been strong when strength was called for. She'd made her way through the snow—albeit with a little goading now and then—and when it came right down it it, she hadn't slowed him down much more than the storm would have done, anyway. He supposed she deserved a bit of respect for that.

So he granted her the respect, but he was feeling something else. He was feeling compassion again, and the strangest need to take her into his arms. She really was a small thing. Sitting there in a sweater and jeans, with her hair—light brown, he saw now, and matted from spending so long under her hood, but still pretty—brushing her shoulders, her head bowed and her arms drawn into herself, she was the embodiment of loneliness. At least, it seemed that way to him. Looking at her, he relived every lonely moment he'd had in his own life, and though he hadn't needed the solace then, he did now.

Gently he pulled up the blanket, which had slipped to the floor. Then he wrapped an arm around her shoulder and drew her against his chest. She didn't melt; her body remained stiff, and her sobs continued to come, but she didn't push him away, and he was glad for that. Holding her made him feel better. And that was all he did, just held her. He didn't stroke her or whisper soft words that he didn't mean. He just held her, just let her feel the solidity of his body and hear the beat of his heart.

After several minutes her sobs subsided, and he could have sworn he felt the slightest relaxation of her body against his. Before he was quite sure, though, she took a deep, shaky breath and made a small movement in search of her freedom. He dropped his arms and sat back on his heels to watch while she gingerly eased herself down on the mattress and drew the baby close.

Her movements were unsteady, not quite coordinated. She was physically hurting, and he could understand that, since he was feeling the same way. Everything that had been close to frozen not long before was beginning to ache—that, in spite of the fact that the warmth from the woodstove felt wonderful.

Lying on her side with an arm draped lightly over the baby, Lily closed her eyes. Quist guessed that she was asleep in less than two minutes, and though he had plenty to do— not the least important of which was to fix something to eat—he sat for a while watching her.

She'd pushed herself to the limit that day, he knew, and though neither of them had had a choice in the matter, he wondered once again whether she'd been up to it. Lying there curled up, with the blanket half-on and half-off, with her hair fallen into her face and smudges visible beneath her eyes, she seemed a far cry from the woman he'd first seen the day before. The sporty car was left behind, her makeup worn off, her fancy clothes, pared down to the basics. She could almost have passed for a ranch girl.

Almost. But not quite.

The baby made a sudden squeak. Quist's eyes flew to her. She was batting the air with all four limbs. He moved closer, wondering what was wrong with her. He fully expected her to start crying any minute, and while he thought that would be a shame, when Lily was finally getting a rest, he wasn't about to save the day by picking her up.

Strangely she didn't start crying, but made another sound, this one the tiniest coo that he almost suspected came out by accident, if the look of surprise on her face was for real. As he watched her, Quist found other things even more surprising.

For one thing, she was even smaller than he'd thought. No longer hidden by the snowsuit, she was wearing a one-piece terry-cloth thing that moved with her. The only point of padding was her diaper, which crinkled softly as she kicked. Though her feet were covered, her hands were free, and smaller, more delicate fingers he'd never seen in his life.

For another, though she didn't have much hair to speak of, she looked like a girl. No doubt, he decided, it was because she was wearing pink and because he *knew* she was a girl. Still, she had the same delicacy to her features, albeit small-scale, as her mother. He couldn't imagine a baby boy looking like that, or if one did, he pitied it.

For a third, she was looking at him as though she possessed some sort of advanced intelligence. She didn't blink. She just stared right at him with eyes that were large and gray. He moved a little to the left; she followed him there. He moved back to the right; so did she. He felt as though he ought to be carrying on some sort of intent conversation with her, but for the life of him, he didn't know what to say—and he could have sworn she knew it, the minx!

Then she sneezed. Her tiny body recoiled along with the small, sweet sound, face puckering, arms and legs flinching. Quist was entranced—until her face stayed puckered and she started to cry.

Lily moved at the sound. She opened her eyes, groggily lifted her head and reached out for the baby's hand, which instinctively curled around her thumb. "Shh," she whispered and closed her eyes again. "Let Mommy rest a little more. Just a little more."

But Nicki wasn't about to do that. She was hungry, and she had no better way to communicate it than to intensify the force of her cries. She proceeded to do just that.

Lily gave a soft moan. She ached all over, and what didn't ache, tingled. Beyond that, she felt totally drained, not at all up to shouldering responsibility. She wanted to *have* a mother right then, not *be* a mother. But the clock couldn't be turned back. And this particular responsibility couldn't be handled by anyone else.

Without rising, she drew Nicki close, unbuttoned her sweater and bared a breast for the child's taking. At the first hint of the nipple's presence, Nicki turned her little head and latched on. In turn, Lily closed her eyes and focused on this small pleasure to counter her larger aches.

Quist hadn't moved. He sat on his heels not far from Lily, his hands splayed on his thighs, his eyes glued to the tableau before him. It was the first time he'd watched her nurse, and though a small amount of the discomfort he'd felt on other occasions remained, something stronger held him in its thrall. He wasn't quite sure what it was—whether it had to do with the bend of Lily's slim legs under the blanket, the graceful line of her back and the curve of the arm that held the baby close, or the peaceful look that had crept over her face. He wondered whether it had to do with the exposure of her breast, which looked full and creamy, or the disappearance of her nipple into the baby's mouth, or the small, sucking motion of that mouth, or the tiny hand that looked so pink on Lily's ivory flesh.

He guessed that it wasn't any one of those things, but several or all of them that contributed to his fascination. The picture before him was very beautiful. It stirred him.

Realization of that stirring was enough to break the spell. Closing his eyes tightly, he hung his head, and, without conscious intent, swayed on his heels against the pain he felt deep inside. It was the pain of sadness, the pain of wanting something and knowing that it was never to be.

The pain lasted for just a minute. In its wake came the refortifying of Quist's defenses—and an anger that those defenses had been breached at all—and the determination that it wouldn't happen again.

4

WHAT THE CABIN LACKED by way of running water and a bathroom, it made up for in food. The kitchen, which consisted of a full wall of shelves and a large sink, contained canned goods ranging from soups and stew to fish, vegetables and fruit. Airtight containers held staples such as sugar, flour and salt. There was a large jar of peanut butter, several smaller jars of wax-sealed jelly that looked to have been home done, and a tin of thick crackers. And there were envelopes of powdered milk and cocoa.

Not bad, Quist decided. If need be, they could stay holed up there, well-fed for a month. Not that he had any intention of doing that. He wanted out, and the sooner the better. He still had Quebec to hit—though whether Lily's little folly would screw that up, too, he didn't know. If he was so late getting to Quebec that Jennifer had run somewhere else, he'd be pissed off. He wasn't sure he'd follow her. Enough was enough. He wanted to be back home, where things were normal.

Taking a handful of crackers from the tin, he sampled one. It was bland and stale, still he chased it down with a second. Intense hunger had a way of humbling even the most discriminating of men, and he'd never been that. Maybe in some things, but not food.

He shot a glance at Lily, thinking to start her eating, too, but her eyes were closed. She was in another world. He had no wish to intrude.

Setting the rest of the crackers within munching distance, he took a large can of stew from the shelf, opened it with the can opener that lay nearby and dumped the contents into a saucepan. When he was satisfied with the way the stew was starting to heat on top of the woodstove, he put on his boots, took a large pot and headed outside to fill it with snow.

He hadn't even reached the door when the cold hit him. It hadn't been as noticeable before, since he'd been so cold himself, but now that he'd warmed up, the contrast was marked. The cabin might have been lovingly used in spring, summer and fall, but he doubted that its owners used it much in winter. If so, they'd have insulated the walls better against storms like this one. Frigid air, even bursts of fine snowflakes were driven by the wind through cracks that the human eye could barely see. That made the temperature by the front walls, where the two cots flanked the door, a good twenty degrees cooler than the air by the woodstove, which stood deeper into the cabin. It was a sure bet that he and Lily would be centering their existence by the latter, and a small space it was, indeed.

On that discouraging note, he slammed out the door.

Lily roused at the noise and looked around just as Nicki was taking a break. Struggling to a sitting position, she laid the baby across her lap and gently burped her, then put her to the other breast.

Moments later Quist returned. He brought with him a fierce gust of wind and a large pot of snow. After brushing himself off, he set the pot on the floor by the woodstove. Once melted, its contents would provide water for drinking, washing and whatever else they wanted. What *he* wanted was a double shot of whiskey. Naturally, it was the only thing the kitchen didn't have.

Ignoring Lily as best he could, he stirred the stew, then put several scoops of snow into a smaller saucepan and set it on to heat for cocoa.

"We lucked out, huh?" Lily said softly.

He shot her a glance, then looked away when he found she was still nursing. Her breast was very much covered to the point where the baby's mouth was attached. Still, the image was there, etched deeply in his mind along with memory of the stirring he'd felt. That stirring meant trouble.

"Lucked out?" He wasn't so sure. There was nothing lucky about being a sap, and if he allowed Lily to get to him, that was just what he'd be. She was a woman, with an agenda of her own. It was totally different from his.

"Warmth. Food. It could have been worse."

"Wait till you see the plumbing."

She looked around, searching the shadows at the perimeter of the room.

"Don't bother," he said. "It's nonexistent. There's an outhouse. The door's half-off, but it serves the purpose." He paused, waiting for her reaction to that bit of news.

If there was dismay on her face, it was lost amid the fatigue. "That's okay," she said quietly—so quietly that he didn't feel any of the satisfaction he'd hoped for. Against his will, he was vaguely concerned.

"How do you feel?"

"Okay."

"Tired?"

"Very."

"Sore."

"A little." It was more than that, but she didn't want to complain. A good night's rest and the soreness would pass, even that in her wrist, which was throbbing. Fortunately it was her left wrist. She could work around it.

"Are you warm enough now?"

"I think so." She glanced at the lower half of her jeans. "These are wet. I'll change when I'm done with Nicki." She kept her head low. "Quist?"

He was wondering what he was supposed to do while she changed. The cabin was a single, open room with neither a divider nor facility for one. His first thought was to watch her, and that angered him. So he snapped, "What?"

At his tone she hesitated, but only for a minute. "I'm sorry—about before. I don't usually fall apart that way, but it's been hard—" Her voice cracked. She took a deep breath. "I've always been one to cry. I cry at everything—books, movies, graduations, weddings, funerals, you name it—but lately it's been worse. It must be post-partum depression, or something."

"Yeah, well . . ."

"Crying is a sign of weakness."

"Who told you that?"

"Jarrod. Over and over and over again."

"He sounds like an asshole."

She raised tentative eyes to his. "I'd have thought you'd agree with him."

"I do in one sense. I hate crying."

She waited for him to go on, brows lifting slightly. He'd have been happy to leave the subject there and then, and might have if it hadn't been for that silent invitation. In its innocence, it was powerful, a challenge to his own sense of truth.

"Crying can be manipulative," he said. "It can be melodramatic and phony as hell. And messy."

Still she waited with that same air of expectancy, and it occurred to him that he was being manipulated without a tear in sight. The thought wasn't terribly reassuring. Still, he was driven to finish his thought.

"But it can also have a positive purpose. Certain of life's circumstances are pretty hefty. At those times, crying can be the expression of honest, gut-wrenching emotion, and in that sense, it's a strength." He paused, his frown deepening at the slight change in her expression. "What's the matter now?"

She shook her head. "Nothing."

"Why are you staring at me like that?" He felt as though she were judging him, and he didn't like it one bit.

She looked away, then back. "I'm surprised, that's all. I didn't expect an answer like that. I mean, it's almost like you've spent time thinking the whole thing through—"

"You didn't expect me to think?"

"It's not that. I didn't expect that you'd—"

"Feel? What do you take me for, an ignorant clod?"

"Of course, not."

"Ah, but I'm a cowboy. I'm not supposed to be a hell of a lot brighter'n my horse."

"You're a *man*," she cried in frustration. "Men aren't usually insightful, or sensitive when it comes to feelings. They don't say things like you just did. They have an image to uphold, and crying doesn't fit the image."

"I didn't say that I cried," he warned.

"See? You say it can be a strength, but still you want to make it clear that you don't do it. That is very male of you."

He shook his head. "Practical. It's practical. I don't cry, because as an outlet it doesn't work for me. I'm not saying it never did, just that I don't do it now."

"You used to cry?"

He shrugged.

"When?"

"I don't know."

"When you were little?"

"Every kid cries. You did. I did." He tossed a hand toward Nicki. "She does."

"But when you were five. Or six or seven. I can't picture you crying then. You're too tough."

"I cried," he argued. He wasn't ashamed of feeling what he had at that point in his life. It showed that he was human, and that he had depth. Suddenly telling her became a matter of pride. "My mother walked out on my dad and me soon after I was born. I didn't miss her at all except for certain times, like birthdays and Christmas and special days at school when all the other kids had mothers visiting. I hated those times. I felt angry and hurt and alone, and I didn't understand any of it. So I used to race home, run down to the basement of the triple-decker we rented, hide behind the furnace where no one would hear me and cry."

Lily's eyes had widened as he spoke. They envisioned a little boy, a confused little boy who wanted something without quite knowing what it was. "That's so sad," she whispered.

But he didn't want her pity. "That's not the point. The point is that I cried because at that time it was the only way I could express what I was feeling. When I got older, I found other ways."

"Like?"

"Like pounding fence posts into the ground, or hacking old cedar stumps to bits, or riding hell-bent for leather to the outer pastures to check on my stock." He took a fast breath. "So don't think I don't think or feel just because I don't cry like you do. I handle my feelings differently, that's all." He stirred the stew with more force than was necessary, and announced sharply, "This is almost ready. When are you going to be done?"

"Soon," Lily said distractedly. She was still thinking of Quist as a little boy, and looking down at Nicki, she felt an awful fear that without a father the child might experience similar pain. "Not if I can help it," she whispered fiercely as she bent low over her. By the time she'd relaxed her grip, Nicki had had enough milk. Lifting her to her shoulder, Lily looked around.

The cabin was a utilitarian affair. A small trestle table flanked by broad benches stood not far from the woodstove. Closer to the front of the cabin were a pair of Adirondack chairs with cushions of a nondescript brown plaid. The front wall held the cots, which doubled as sofas, she guessed, and just around the corner from those were two crudely-fashioned dressers.

With an effort and a small, involuntary groan, she managed to get to her feet. Her legs still felt foreign—stiff and shaky at the same time, and weak—but they did respond to commands of her brain, enough to get her to one of the dressers. The drawers held towels and more blankets, but she wasn't interested in their contents. Finding an empty one, she used her right hand to haul it completely out and lug it toward the woodstove, while she kept her left arm curved protectively around Nicki.

Dropping the drawer on the mattress, she lined it with the blanket Quist had put around her, then double-lined it with the softer receiving blanket that she took from the baby's bag. Nicki had burped by then, and Lily gently lowered her to the makeshift crib. The fit was fine. Eyes on her mother, the baby gently waved her arms and made such sweet gurgling sounds that Lily couldn't help but lean forward and laugh. Nor could she help but congratulate herself on her inventiveness. To date, Quist had been the one in charge. It was time she took over some, at least where she and her child were concerned.

Bearing that in mind, she forced herself back to her feet and once again left the circle of the woodstove's warmth.

The floor by the door was littered with all they'd discarded when they'd first come in. Most of it was wet, now that the snow had melted, and she knew that anything that wasn't spread out or hung to dry would stay wet. So she picked up first her boots, then Quist's and stood them against the side of the chair facing the fire. Then she went back for more.

"What's wrong with your hand?" Quist asked. He was leaning against the trestle table, watching her.

"Nothing."

"You're favoring it like it hurts."

She shrugged off the problem. "I landed on it when I fell, but it's just a sprain. It'll be fine."

"Let me see." He started toward her, but she held up a fast hand to stop him.

"It's *fine. Really.*"

At the insistence in her tone, he backed off, but he continued to watch. His mouth twisted when he saw her pick up the fur coat. He should have known she'd worry about it, and he supposed he couldn't blame her. It was worth a mint. Still, she had quite a time spreading it out on the bare metal springs of the cot whose mattress he'd moved. She made a show of using her left hand, but her right was the one that did all the work. Likewise when it came to draping her parka over the back of a chair. When she bent to pick up her wool coat, he'd seen enough. "Leave it," he barked, turning away.

Lily, who had been concentrating on the mechanics of the chore, whirled around. "What?"

"I said, leave it. You can pick up later. Supper's ready."

Supper. The word alone made her mouth water, but she'd been in the outer parts of the cabin long enough to be acutely aware of her legs. "Give me a minute. I have to change."

Dragging her bag onto the cot, she fished inside until she found the warmest wool slacks she'd brought. Then she paused, wondering where she was supposed to change. She was in the darker part of the cabin, still Quist could see plenty.

"Do it there," he told her, as though he'd read her mind. But his voice was more impatient than smug. "I won't look."

When she glanced over her shoulder, he was turning away. Determined to seize the moment, she quickly reached for the top button of her jeans. But what was simply done with two hands wasn't quite as simple with one. She pushed, pulled and tugged, but the metal button wouldn't slide through its hole. When she tried to use the fingers of her left hand to anchor the denim, the only thing to come from the effort was a low moan of pain.

Clamping down on her lower lip, she worked feverishly at the fabric until, at last, the button was freed. But there were still four more. With a whispered cry of frustration, she went to work on the second.

"Let me see your hand," Quist demanded.

Lily jumped. He was right behind her, then beside her. "You weren't supposed to be looking," she protested.

"You were taking forever. The stew's done, and I'm hungry. Let me see your hand." He reached for it before she could pull away, and then the only thing she could do to minimize the pain was to move right along with the hand. That brought her flush against Quist. Leaning over her, he began to examine her wrist.

Despite his gentleness, she sucked in her breath.

"Hurt?" he asked.

"Yes," she whispered.

He moved his fingers, prodding as lightly as he could while still assessing the damage. "Here?"

She gasped.

"A lot?" he asked.

"Enough."

He probed one more spot, using his thumbs to explore. This time, she would have jumped sky-high at the pain if he hadn't had her anchored to him with his elbows. "I think you've broken the wrist," he announced.

She shook her head against his chest and said in a shaky voice, "Oh, no. It's not broken."

"How do you know?"

"I know. It's not broken."

"I felt it, Lily. That last time, I felt the bone moving. And see how swollen it is." Putting his palms under hers, he held her hands side by side. The difference between them was marked.

"It's sprained. That's all. If I pamper it a little, it'll heal just fine."

"It'll take more than pampering. It should be immobilized and elevated. I'll have to splint it."

"But it's not broken," she insisted, tipping her head back this time to look into his face.

He'd never seen such pleading or such fear, and he was touched so quickly that he didn't have time to tell himself that he didn't want to be touched. "I'm not going to cut it off. Just splint it."

"But if it's broken, I can't use it," she said in a small, high voice. "And I have to use it. I have to be able to take care of Nicki. She has no one else, just me."

"She's a little thing. You'll be able to handle her fine."

"Not if you do something to my hand."

"You're the one who did something. I'm only going to try to fix it."

She looked down at the hand and repeated firmly, "It's just a sprain. No big deal. Leave it alone, and it'll be better in the morning. You'll see."

"Leave it alone, and it'll be worse," he argued, then deliberately gentled his voice. She felt so small and vulnerable, leaning against him like she was. "I'm telling you, Lily, I know about these things. Bones break lots in my line of work. Ignore them, and you're in big trouble. If the bone you've broken knits wrong, you'll have a choice between surgery to rebreak and reset it, in which case you'll be in a cast even longer, or a permanently bum wrist." He paused and tipped his head, coaxing, "All I'm suggesting is that you let me immobilize it until we reach civilization. You can have it X-rayed then, and you'll find out for sure whether or not it's broken. If it's not, good. You'll have taken a precaution, that's all."

Lily was torn. His deep voice was so reassuring, his body so large and warm and supportive, that she wanted to say, "Yes, yes, do whatever you want, take the responsibility, I'm so tired." Still, she didn't want to believe that anything was seriously wrong with her wrist. When and if they were rescued, she had so much to do. She had to finish the drive north, find a place to stay, a job, a bank, a supermarket, a pediatrician, day-care—the list went on. A broken wrist would complicate things horribly.

"It isn't broken," she stated in a last-ditch attempt to believe it.

Removing his hands from hers, Quist held them up and took a step back. "Okay. It's not broken. I guess you know best." She was a big girl, he decided. He couldn't force her to do something she didn't want to do. It was her wrist, her future. If she wanted to mess it up, so be it.

Without another word on the subject, he returned to the stove and began to dish out the stew. After a minute, Lily followed him. He sent her a scowl.

"I thought you were changing your pants."

"I'll do it later," she mumbled.

He stared at her averted face for a minute, then swore and dropped the spoon back into the pan of stew. "You'll do it later, hah. You won't do it later, any more than you'll do it now, because you can't manage those stupid buttons with only one hand." Taking her firmly by her good arm, he ushered her back to her bag. "What in the hell possessed you to buy button-fly jeans, anyway? They went out when zippers came in, for one good reason. When a man wants his pants open, he wants them open fast."

Lily would have gasped at what he said if he hadn't said it so factually. "Button-fly jeans are in fashion," she offered meekly. He made a sound that told her what he thought of fashion. When he began pulling things from her bag, she cried, "What are you doing?"

"I thought I saw you pack a pair of sweatpants in here. Where are they?"

She had her hand on them quickly. They were pink, rather than gray, which was probably why he hadn't spotted them. "What do you want with my sweatpants?"

"I don't want them," he growled, squatting before her. "*You* do." Before the words were out, he was working on her pants.

She tried to stop him. "What are you *doing*?"

He pushed her hand away. "Undoing these. You can't manage it yourself, and there's no other way to get the damned pants off." With half of the buttons undone, he paused and looked up at her. "You're going to have to take them off sooner or later, whether it's here or in that outhouse. Better here—take my word for it." He returned to his work. "And better now. You need dry and warm, not wet and cold." He tugged at one stubborn button. "Besides, these jeans are skin-tight, and you haven't eaten all day. Once you've had a little of that stew, there'll be even less room to maneuver the buttons."

Lily turned beet red. "I know. My stomach isn't as flat as it used to be." All the buttons were undone. He began to work the denim down her legs. She clutched his shoulder for balance, speaking quickly to cover her nervousness. "I've been doing sit-ups. That helps. It's much better than it was at first. I only gained twenty-three pounds during the pregnancy," she balanced on one foot, while he freed the other, "and all but the last five are gone, but those five pounds don't want to move." She shifted her balance. "Some women are lucky and have no problem. I guess I'm not one of them."

Quist tossed the jeans aside. He wanted to say something about Lily's propensity for problems, but the words didn't come. His attention was focused on the five pounds she'd been talking about. Only he couldn't seem to see them. He saw a slim waist and hips, and a stomach that was ever-so-gently rounded as to be utterly feminine. She wore a pair of white bikini panties, nylon with lace that dipped in a V beneath her navel and was a perfect foil for that soft, gentle rounding.

She was lovely. Soft, gentle, feminine. Unable to help himself, he let his eyes run down her legs. They were slender but shapely and sheathed in the same ivory hue as her stomach and her breasts. He curved a hand around her heel and skimmed it lightly up over her calf, past the back of her knee and her thigh to come to a whisper-soft halt just under her bottom.

That was when he realized what he was doing. It was when he noticed the fine tremor in his hand, and when he saw the movement at Lily's middle that reflected her own quickened breathing.

His eyes met hers, which were wide with something that wasn't quite fear, wasn't quite surprise, wasn't quite desire but had elements of all three. Awareness. That was what he saw. In the instant when he'd touched her, she'd become aware of him as a man.

Her hand, which had never left his shoulder, was gripping it more tightly. At the same time, he caught an almost imperceptible shake of her head.

So she didn't want it, either, he realized and felt a glimmer of relief. If there had to be an attraction between them, at least it was mutually unwanted. It wasn't that he didn't trust himself—though he supposed he didn't. When he was attracted to a woman, he usually followed the attraction to its limits. Sometimes he did so against his better judgment, but if the woman was willing, his brain didn't have much of a chance against the demands of his body. He was glad Lily wasn't willing.

Tearing his eyes from hers, he reached for the pink sweatpants. He knew he should get up and walk away, but he was determined to finish what he'd started. In the process of doing that, the first thing he touched was her damp socks. Reaching again, this time into his own duffel, he replaced those damp socks with a pair of his own clean, dry, wool socks. He figured it was some compensation for thinking lascivious thoughts. Besides, there was nothing at all sexy about a lady wearing wool socks that were way too big, or about a lady wearing pink sweatpants over those socks.

"There," he said when he'd finished, but he had to clear his throat before he spoke again. "The elastic waist is easier."

Rising to his full height, he had to stifle a moan. He was stiff in more ways than one. Peeved at that, he crossed the room and finished spooning stew into the bowls.

It was a minute before Lily followed. She spent that minute trying to understand the warm curling she'd felt inside when Quist had seen her undressed. And when he'd touched her. That had been incredible. The feeling had been so unexpected, but good. She couldn't deny that. Of course, good was all there was to it—a moment's pleasure from physical contact with another person, flesh on flesh, a deeper warmth. It wouldn't go any further than that. It was the circumstances, that was all.

Feeling a slight chill, she took a pair of sneakers from her bag and, perching on the edge of one of the Adirondack chairs, tried to put them on. The bulk of Quist's wool socks would have made the task next to impossible even if she'd had both hands to work with, but without both hands, she couldn't even come close. About all she could do with her left hand was to pick at the laces, and ineffectually, at that. Rather than make an issue of her wrist again, she gave up the struggle.

Shoving the sneakers out of sight, she took several small, bright, rubber toys from the baby's bag, put them on the trestle table and went to get Nicki. She managed it by sliding her right hand under the baby and using her left elbow to help. Grateful that she could do that much, she put Nicki on her stomach on a receiving blanket on the table.

Quist set down the bowls of stew, deposited the tin of crackers nearby and sat opposite Lily. If there was a lingering awkwardness from what had happened before, it quickly passed. Hunger and its assuagement was foremost in their minds. They ate in a silence broken only by Lily's occasional soft chatter to the baby. Quist refilled each of their bowls, and they efficiently went through seconds.

Lily was still savoring the very last of the stew, thinking that nothing canned had ever tasted so good, particularly when she'd been growing up and canned food was frequent fare, when Quist set a mug before her.

"Milk," he said. "Powdered. Probably tastes lousy, but I think you need it."

She did. Since midway through her pregnancy, she'd been drinking several glasses a day. Now, nursing Nicki, it was more important than ever, yet she hadn't had a drop in a day and a half. She didn't care how the powdered version tasted. For Nicki's sake, she'd drink it.

It wasn't half-bad, she found. She was thirsty anyway, and it quenched that thirst. Quist was drinking cocoa. She'd have loved to have had some of that, but she didn't dare.

Stacking the bowls, she gave a vague look toward the sink. "I'm not sure how to do this."

"Never roughed it?"

"Why are there spigots if there isn't any running water?"

"There is in the summer. Whoever owns this place drained the pipes before winter so they wouldn't freeze and burst. Makes sense."

She supposed it did, but that didn't solve the immediate problem. Of course, the immediate problem was exacerbated by the pain she felt each time she moved her left hand, but she was going to have to learn to work around that, too.

Quist watched her face. He could practically read the thoughts going through her mind, particularly since she was gingerly holding that left hand at her waist. It needed to be splinted, and badly. But she was going to have to reach that conclusion herself. He wondered how long it would take her.

Though his first instinct was to do the cleanup himself and let her concentrate on the baby, he sat back leisurely drinking his cocoa. "There's a basin by the sink," he said. "Fill it with the water that's left on the stove. Add enough cold water from what's on the floor so you don't burn yourself. Soap and stuff is by the basin."

It sounded nearly as simple as it was. Lily managed to clean everything they'd used for dinner, and conveniently there was a draining rack by the sink, so she didn't have to worry about drying, which she guessed would be more difficult.

When she was done, she felt buoyed. Returning to the table, she sat down, put her face on eye level with the baby and said, "How's it going, Nicki?"

Nicki, who'd been nudging a soft plastic ring in the general vicinity of her mouth, lifted her head and looked at Lily with round eyes that expressed excitement at having her mother's attention again.

"What a bright little girl," Lily whispered in praise. Smiling, she ran her hand over the baby's soft brown hair.

"What does she do?" Quist asked.

Lily looked up. "What do you mean?"

"Is this it? She sleeps, eats and cries, lies around kicking her arms and legs and making faces?"

Lily wasn't offended. Quist just didn't know. Two months before, she'd probably have asked the same question. So it was easy to be patient. "She looks around. She absorbs what she sees and tries to make sense out of it. She responds to the people she's with." Lowering her head again, Lily said in a soft, mommy voice, "Isn't that so, Nicki? There's so much to see in the world, even in this dark, old cabin. There's the sound of the wind and snow outside, and the buzz of the fire and the light from the lamp. There's my face and his face and the table and your toys—" She broke off, because Nicki grinned, and it was such a delightful thing to see that Lily laughed. When she reached for the baby to hug her, though, the laugh ended with a sharp cry. Without thinking, she'd tried to use her left hand. It was a mistake.

Coming to her feet, she did manage to get Nicki into her arms, but the hug she gave her was selfish, more to comfort herself than anything else.

"Your face went white just then," Quist informed her.

"Thanks."

"It's going to get worse."

"No. I just forgot for a minute. When Nicki smiles, I forget about everything else."

Quist hadn't seen the smile, because he'd been studying Lily's face at the time. He'd been trying to understand how a woman who looked tired and bedraggled could suddenly start to beam. He supposed it was what she said, that Nicki made her forget about other things, but having never had an experience like it, he couldn't quite understand. He'd never been so caught up with another human being that he'd forgotten who he was, what he was doing and why.

"Does she smile often?" he asked.

Cradling Nicki between her body and her left arm, with the injured hand angled away, she used her right to tease the baby's chin. "More and more now. Her first smiles came and went so fast that I wasn't really sure what I'd seen, or whether it was a real smile or a gas pain. Lately the smiles come at appropriate times." Lily grinned and her voice went up. "Like now."

He saw it that time, toothless and wide, and there was something about it that made him smile inside. She looked so happy, Nicki did, so happy in such a wholehearted, innocent way that it would have been impossible for him to do anything else. When her smile disappeared, he was sorry and found himself watching closely to see if it would come again.

It did. So did several others, all in response to Lily's coaxing and cajoling. In time, though, as was inevitable, Nicki tired. Her little face remained serious. Then she began to squirm and grimace. Lily did her best to restore her good mood, hoping, among other things, to prolong her wakeful period as much as possible so that she'd sleep longer through the night. But the whimpers came next, and when they persisted, Lily knew she had to do something.

Changing a diaper, particularly those of the disposable, painless variety, was a relatively easy chore. Lily had changed dozens in the past five weeks. She felt she'd become an expert.

Always before, though, she'd had two hands, and never before had she had an audience. If she'd thought ahead, she'd probably have changed the baby in her drawer on the floor, where her one-handed awkwardness would have been hidden. But she didn't think beyond the ease of changing the baby on the table, and once she'd managed to scoop up the diaper bag from the shadows, juggle both the bag and Nicki, then deposit Nicki on the receiving blanket, she wasn't about to lift her again so fast.

So with Quist watching, she went about the task. Unsnapping the lower part of the terry jumpsuit was easy enough to do with one hand, as was freeing the baby's tiny feet. Lifting the jumpsuit out of the way without lifting the baby was a little tougher. Lily pushed and tugged. She tried to act natural doing it, though she was sure that she looked incompetent, which was very much how she felt. But the diaper had to be changed, and there was no one to do it but her.

She kept at it. Talking soft gibberish to Nicki, which was what she always did when she changed her, she ever so carefully held one part of the diaper down with the very tops of the fingers of her left hand, while she tore first one tape, then the other. Thanking her lucky stars that the baby was only wet, she lifted the two little feet in her right hand and pushed the diaper out of the way with the side of her left.

That brought a closed-mouth moan.

"Lily," Quist warned.

"It's okay," she said quickly.

"Each time you do something like that, it makes it worse."

"It's sore. That's all."

"You're risking greater damage."

"Oh, hush. You're just trying to make your point."

"Damn right, I am. That wrist is broken—"

"Sprained. It'll be fine," she said with determination. Drawing the new diaper close, she lifted Nicki's feet again and nudged the diaper under her. Though she didn't moan that time, tiny dots of perspiration broke out on her nose. Weak-kneed, she lowered herself to the bench.

"What's wrong?" Quist asked, concerned by her pallor.

Lily took a premoistened towelette from its pack. "I wish I could bathe her. It's been so long."

He was relieved that was all. "She looks pretty clean to me."

"She is, I suppose." Using her one good hand, she managed to wipe the baby's bottom.

Quist watched everything she did. He wasn't feeling as smug as he had before. She wasn't giving in to the pain like he thought she would, and he was beginning to really worry about her wrist. But aside from that worry, he watched out of pure curiosity. Without her sleeper, Nicki was smaller than ever. He couldn't say that she was scrawny, because she looked healthy and well fed, still she was small. He doubted her foot was as big as his thumb. Looking at her, he found it hard to believe she would grow up one day to have the kind of gentle, womanly curves her mother did.

Annoyed that he'd even thought that, he scowled. Seconds later, when Lily liberally coated the baby's bottom with Vaseline, he said on a note of distaste, "That looks like the most uncomfortable thing in the world. Who wants to go around with a greasy butt?"

"A baby who doesn't want a rash. The Vaseline protects her." Lily arched a brow his way. "She's not riding a horse, Quist."

That shut him up, but it was a short-lived victory for Lily. Securing the new diaper on Nicki was a trial, as was getting her dressed again. By the time she was done, Lily was frazzled and her wrist was worse.

"What now?" Quist asked. He hadn't moved an inch, still sat at the table with his forearms flat and his mouth set.

"I'm going to bed," Lily answered. She didn't know what else to do. She was feeling lots of things—annoyed that he'd watched her struggle without offering to help, afraid that he was right about her wrist, fearful that the storm had worsened and that they'd be stuck in the cabin for days. Mostly, though, she was feeling exhausted. She hadn't done more than doze the night before, and now, with a full stomach after a day that had been endless and tense, she wanted the blissful escape of sleep.

First, though, she had to put Nicki into her blanket sleeper. She did it with the baby in the drawer this time, still it was an ordeal. Between the frustration and the pain, Lily was near tears by the time she finished. Sheer force of will kept her from breaking down again—that, and Nicki's precious face looking up at her from amid the blankets.

"You're such a love," she whispered, leaned low and kissed the baby's soft cheek. The contact felt so good that she stayed there for a minute. For another minute she actually debated having Nicki sleep with her on the mattress. She wanted to hold—or be held—anything to ward off the fear she felt.

Given the tender state of her wrist, it was a bad idea, she decided. So she took a deep breath and stood. With her back to Quist and her head down, she said, "I have to use the outhouse. Where is it?"

Quist closed his eyes briefly, only then admitting to the suffering he'd felt watching Lily try to manage Nicki with one hand. Now she had to use the bathroom, which meant putting on boots and a coat, then taking them off again. He'd wanted to make a point before, but he just wasn't enough of a bastard to carry it to the extreme.

"Come on," he said and went for his boots.

Lily grew alarmed. "Uh, you don't have to go out. Just tell me where—is it to the right or the left—how far away—"

"It's wild out there."

She could hear it. The wind had been howling around the corners of the cabin since they'd arrived and showed no sign of letting up. Still, she didn't want Quist taking her to the bathroom. It was embarrassing.

"I'm taking you."

"That's not necessary."

"I think it is," he said firmly. He knelt and held her boot.

Lily stared at the boot for a minute, but that was all it took for her to realize that, as had been the case with changing her pants, embarrassment was impractical. Gripping his shoulder, she pushed her foot in. After he'd held the second boot in the same manner, he held her coat for her. He was duly patient when it came to the left hand, which she took more time easing in.

When he tossed on his own coat, she made a final plea. "I'd feel better knowing you were here with Nicki."

He shot a fast glance at the baby, but she was little more than a silent bundle of blankets in her drawer. "You think she might get up and run off?"

"Of course not, but—"

"Someone may come and abduct her while we're gone? A kidnapper? In this blizzard?"

"What if something happens, like a spark coming out of the woodstove—"

"I've been watching that woodstove since I lit it, and it doesn't send out sparks. It's perfectly safe."

"Still—"

"Look at it this way," he said with a tired sigh. "The chances of something happening to Nicki alone in here are far less than something happening to you alone out there. So I'll come—unless you're planning to spend two hours in the outhouse, in which case, thanks, but I will stay here."

"I'll only be a minute."

"That's what I thought. Let's go." Pushing the Stetson onto his head, he took the hurricane lamp and her arm and drew her out the door.

The storm was as wild as he'd said. Snow was heavy underfoot and overhead, a fury of bright white dots whipping around in the light of the lamp at the mercy of the wind. She ducked her head against the cold, stinging flakes and let Quist forge the way. She heard him swear, or thought she heard him, though with her hood over her ears and the thunder of the wind she couldn't be sure. But she was glad he'd come. Even if she'd known where she was going, she wouldn't have liked being out there alone. It was dark and cold and wet and scary.

The outhouse stood a dozen yards behind the cabin in what seemed a never-never land of snow. By the time they reached it, Lily wouldn't have cared if Quist had come inside. But he shoved her in with the lantern, yelled, "Hurry," and pulled the door closed.

She was as quick as she could be, given her hand, the cold, and the utter foreignness of the place. She didn't stop to look around; she was afraid of what she'd see. So she simply relieved herself, thanked God that Quist had had the foresight to put her in sweatpants, straightened her clothing and left.

Not about to waste the trip, Quist took his turn while Lily stood outside, huddling against the snow-encrusted wood with her arms wrapped around herself and her face buried in her coat. As soon as he came out, they trudged back to the cabin. The return should have been easier, since they'd already made tracks, but the sheer volume of snow worked against them.

Once inside, Lily went straight to Nicki, who was sound asleep, none the worse for the few minutes she'd spent alone. Quist made no comment, but helped her take her things off, then took off his own and dropped into one of the Adirondack chairs.

Taking a pillow and blanket from another of the dresser drawers, Lily lay down on the mattress in front of the stove, shivered under the blanket until the cold from outside had left her, then closed her eyes. She felt bone tired, more so than she could ever remember feeling. But sleep didn't come. Her wrist hurt. She shifted from one side to the other, from her back to her stomach, but there wasn't any escape from the pain. It was relentless, stretching each minute to an agonizing extreme. She tried to will it away, but Quist's words kept echoing in her mind.

"It's broken...I felt it...I felt the bone moving...see how swollen it is... it should be immobilized and elevated."

Shifting her head to one side of the pillow, she propped her wrist on the other. He'd said to elevate it, and that was the one thing she could do without much effort. It was also, she realized after what seemed another eternity of trying to sleep, not doing as much as she'd hoped. The throbbing went on.

"That wrist is broken . . . you're only risking greater damage . . . if the bone knits wrong."

Sitting up, she eyed the wrist as though it were an old friend that had turned traitor. It looked guilty—fat and ugly. And broken. There. She admitted it. But admitting it didn't make the pain go away.

She looked over her shoulder at Quist. He was slouched in the low chair with his legs outstretched, his fingers loosely laced over his middle and his head back against the slats. At first she thought he was asleep. Then she caught the tiny flicker of light reflected in his eyes, and she knew he was looking at her.

"Can you do something?" she asked defeatedly.

"About what?"

"My wrist."

"Not much to do for a sprain," he said, but she heard the challenge in his voice.

She lowered her head. "I can't sleep. It really hurts. I think you're right. It may be broken. I don't want it to be, but what I want isn't always what I get." She raised her eyes to his. "Please."

Quist was out of his chair in a minute, silently cursing himself for making her spell out what she wanted. He didn't like hearing her beg. Somehow it didn't seem right. From what she'd told him, well apart from her wrist, things hadn't gone her way much. If she'd been stubborn before, it had been out of fear. From what he'd seen of her, she wasn't naturally mulish.

"Go sit at the table," he said. He went to the far corner of the room where the dry logs were stored.

Lily wondered what he was doing, but she did her wondering from the table. She watched him take several somethings from the corner, then go back to their bags and get a pair of socks from hers and a shirt from his. She was looking nervous by the time he joined her, which prompted him to explain exactly what he was going to do.

"These are pieces of shingle. I saw them when I took wood for the stove. Someone must have done some repair work on the roof last summer and left the remnants there." He took one of her socks, which were long and cotton, stretched the neck enough to get the piece of shingle going, then shimmied it inside. "They're fiberglass, so they'll be rigid enough to work as a splint without being heavy." He repeated the process with the second piece, then began to tear strips from his shirt.

Lily couldn't believe he was ruining a perfectly good shirt. "Wait, there must be something of mine—"

But he ignored her. "These will hold the whole thing together. You won't be able to move your wrist, which is how we want it." Swinging a leg over the bench, he came down behind Lily. With an arm on either side of her, he was positioned to work on her hand as though it were his own. "I'll have to touch it again to make sure it's okay," he warned. His voice was low but gentle, his breath fanning her temple.

Lily steeled herself for the pain. When it came, she bit her lip and leaned back into him. It was as though one part of her had to escape his prodding, though she didn't move her hand. It was also a move toward a haven that promised warmth and strength.

As gently as he could, Quist continued to probe his way through the swelling to feel the bone that was broken and make sure it was straight. He knew the discomfort he was causing, and again wished for that double shot of whiskey, though not for himself this time. Lily did her best not to make a sound, and except for sharp little gasps when the pain was at its worst, she succeeded. But he could feel the way she pressed back against him, leaning away from the pain, and the way she clutched the table with her good hand and the way she was beginning to tremble. At one point, when she seemed particularly tense, she pressed her face to his arm. He wet his lips and probed on.

"I think that's it," he murmured when he was satisfied that he had the bone aligned. Carefully he slid one of the sock-covered shingles under her hand. He put the second shingle on top, then bound and secured the cotton strips. "I've left your fingers hanging out. You'll be able to use them a little once the swelling goes down."

"When will that be?" she asked. Her face was no longer buried against his sleeve, but her voice was thin. It would have told him she hurt even if he didn't already know.

He rested his hands beside hers, making no move to get up. "As soon as tomorrow, if you keep it raised. The point is to elevate it above your heart so the blood runs away."

"When will it feel better?"

"Tomorrow or the next day, if I've done it right. As long as the bone is aligned and you can't move it, there should be steady improvement. I may have to tighten these strips once the swelling goes down, but that's no big deal."

"Fine for you to say. You're not the one in agony."

He almost wished he were, he felt so badly for her just then. "Got any aspirin?"

"No."

"There's a first-aid kit on one of the shelves." It was a small pack that didn't look capable of containing much more than Band-Aids and disinfectant. But it was worth a try. "Maybe it has aspirin, or something stronger."

"No," she said quickly. "I don't want anything."

"It would help with the pain."

"I can bear the pain as long as I know it's not permanent."

"It's not permanent," he assured her and continued to hold her gently. The tension he'd felt in her body while he'd been working was beginning to drain away, leaving her limp and pliant. She conformed nicely to his frame. While he wasn't sure it was wise of him to appreciate something like that, he knew he'd stay exactly where he was until she showed signs of wanting to move.

After sitting for another minute with her head lolled back against his chest, she slowly drew herself forward. "I should let you sleep."

"I'll sleep later."

"Then I should let me sleep."

It was what she needed most, he knew. He also knew that he wouldn't sleep until she did. Leaving the bench, he went back to the dressers and took out another pillow and three more blankets. He returned to the woodstove just as Lily was checking on Nicki.

"Sleeping?"

She nodded. "I don't know for how long. It could be another hour, or five."

"Then you'd better try to get whatever rest you can now."

She nodded again, but she stayed where she was, sitting on the edge of the mattress with her splinted hand carefully placed on her thigh. Her eyes were soft with fatigue when she looked up at him. "Where will you be?"

He shrugged. "I'll sit here a little, then bring over the other mattress."

She studied her hand for a minute, then looked up again. "Thank you for doing this."

"How does it feel?"

"It still hurts."

He imagined that would go on for a while yet, and since she wouldn't take aspirin, the only other thing he could do was to elevate her hand and try to give her a little relief that way. Without thinking of the absurdity of it, he dragged one of the Adirondack chairs forward, propped a pillow against it and sat down on the floor. Then he took Lily's pillow, put it against his stomach and gestured for her to lie down.

Lily wasn't thinking of the absurdity of it, either. She was remembering how nice it was to be close to Quist's body.

She wanted more of that comfort. It would be better than aspirin, she knew.

Crossing to where he sat, she put her head on the pillow and her splint on the blanket he folded on his knee. She felt him cover her with the third blanket, but she'd already closed her eyes, and she had no intention of spoiling the moment by uttering so much as another thank-you. Just before she fell asleep, she imagined she felt a hand smooth her hair back from her cheek. She held the gesture to her until exhaustion took it and all else.

5

BY THE TIME Nicki stirred, Lily and Quist had shifted to the mattress. They were tucked against each other with Lily in front, nearest the woodstove. Her wrist was still elevated. Quist had woken periodically to make sure of that, and though the wrist still ached, the throbbing had eased. She'd actually been sleeping quite soundly when she'd heard the first of Nicki's tiny cries.

Maternal instinct had awoken her then, a second sense that registered certain sounds while overlooking others. Not being a mother, Quist was without benefit of that instinct. The first he knew of anything amiss was when the softness that had been pressed against him stirred, then inched away. He was slow to realize what was happening, but once he did, he came quickly awake.

"Don't lift her," he said suddenly and loudly.

About to do just that, Lily jumped. She was sure she'd left him asleep. "I have to take her out to feed her," she explained. She returned her attention to Nicki, who wasn't pleased with the delay, but she'd no sooner freed the fussing infant from her blanket than Quist materialized on the opposite side of the drawer.

He was hunkered down, hands poised, voice all business, if a bit groggy. "Tell me what to do."

He was so earnest about it that Lily couldn't help but stare. "You can't feed her, Quist."

"I know that, Lily," he mocked, "but I can get her up and put her in your arms. There's a reason why I made the effort of splinting your wrist, and I didn't have fun doing it, no matter what you think. So let's give the damn thing a chance to heal, huh?" He looked at Nicki again. "Now what do I do? What do I grab?"

Lily felt suddenly light-headed. She figured it had something to do with sleeping so soundly and waking abruptly. She wondered if it had to do with sleeping with Quist. As a compromise she decided it had to do with simple relief that he'd offered to help. Between that light-headedness and the absolutely precious look of intensity on his face, she wanted to laugh. She knew better.

"Slide one hand behind her head and neck, and the other under her bottom. Head and neck. That's right. There, she's fine."

"Why's she screaming?"

"Because she's hungry." She held out her arms.

But Quist kept staring at the bundle in his hands. "She doesn't like the way I'm holding her."

"She likes it just fine." Just as she'd known not to laugh, Lily knew what to say. She was no fool. Quist's offer of help was a godsend. She wasn't about to offend him by telling him he was holding the baby like she was a sacrifice to a pagan god, though the image was apt. He did look half-heathen, dark and mussed and badly in need of a shave, and his arms were tense. "You can relax your hands a little. They're big and she's small—they'll support her without much effort. That's right."

"She's still crying."

Again Lily reached for her. "She wants milk." When he still made no move to hand Nicki over, she lowered her arm and said, "Try bringing her in a little closer to your body. She likes to feel sheltered. There's a comfort in that." As Lily knew from personal experience. "Ah, see? She's quieting down."

"Not all the way. I'm still doing something wrong."

"No, you're not."

"She's uncomfortable with me."

Lily wanted to say that Nicki was wet and hungry and would be uncomfortable with *anyone* who held her just then, but in fact she was crying less loudly than she'd been a minute before. "Hold her like she's a football."

He was horrified by that idea. "Are you kidding?"

"No. You know how they do it when they've got the ball and they're running down the field? Well, shift her around a little so her head's kind of tucked into your elbow."

"How do I do that without dropping her?"

"Slide the hand that's under her head down her back so that your arm keeps supporting her head."

"It'll wobble if I don't, won't it?" he said, but he was following her direction and there wasn't a bit of a wobble.

"That's it. Now ease her up into the crook of your elbow. There." Inordinately pleased, she sat back on her heels. "Perfect. You can even take away the other hand. She's very comfortable there."

Indeed, she was. She'd stopped crying altogether, and although her little mouth was set in a way that threatened she might start in again at any time, she simply looked up at Quist.

He made a small, weighing motion with his arm. "She's very light."

"She's very little."

"Littler than most babies?"

"Littler than some, but none are real big at this age."

He made the small, lifting motion again. "This isn't so bad."

"What did you expect?"

"I don't know. I thought maybe she'd squirm right out of my hands. Know what I'd feel like if that happened and she fell on the floor?"

Lily had asked herself the same question dozens of times in the past five weeks. "She won't."

Nicki continued to study Quist with eyes that looked large and round in her face. Only her hands moved. They were linked in a random way that kept shifting, one tiny index finger on a knuckle, then a pinky around a wrist, then a thumb in a palm. Intrigued, Quist followed the changes.

"Does she know she's doing that?"

"She knows she's touching something that's reassuring and warm. Does she know it's her own hand? Probably not."

"She looks like she does. She looks like she knows a whole lot more than we think she does."

Lily felt a swell of pride, but said nothing. She thought Nicki was brilliant. That didn't mean she was going to boast about it to strangers.

Then again, Quist wasn't really a stranger. Not anymore. She didn't know the details of his life, didn't know what kind of ranch he had or how many men he employed or why he'd been heading for Quebec, but she had a feeling that she knew things about him that other people didn't. She knew that there was a gentle side beneath the gruffness, a caring side beneath the indifference. She knew that though he claimed to dislike women, he didn't like seeing one hurt, and that his aversion to babies wasn't so much aversion as fear, and that though one part of him didn't want to, he liked physical closeness a lot. What else could explain the way he'd chosen to sit when he'd tended her wrist, or the way he'd held her while she'd fallen asleep, or the way he'd kept her curled against him after that, or even the way he was holding the baby now. He still wasn't entirely comfortable with it, but he didn't rush to hand her back.

He was, Lily decided, an interesting man. She'd taken one look at him in the snowstorm and labeled him a cowboy, but there was much more to him than a Stetson. He had a depth that few of the men she'd known possessed. Thirty-six hours—not even that—she'd spent with him, and together they'd run through a gamut of emotions. Still she had a feeling that she'd only seen a few of his layers.

Strange, she mused as she continued to study him, but that top layer had changed since they'd met. She hadn't thought him particularly attractive at first. He'd been too large, too dark, too forbidding. She saw him differently now. Beneath the bulk of his outer clothing, he was well built. Though his shoulders were broad, they tapered to a lean waist and hips and long, strong legs. And while his face was shadowed by a two-day stubble, he didn't look darker, so much as rugged. He had high cheekbones and eyes that weren't coal black, as she'd originally thought, but softer, rich like sable, warm when the defensive walls inside him began to melt. They were doing that now, and he wasn't looking at the baby. He was looking at her, in a way that said they shared something special.

She'd never seen that kind of look in a man's eyes before. God knew Jarrod had never looked at her that way. It made her heart beat faster and her blood heat and her breath trip over itself before rushing on.

In that rush, with her eyes still on Quist's, she whispered, "Maybe I'd better feed her. It's still the middle of the night. I've been trying to teach her that I won't play with her when it's dark. That's the only way she'll learn to sleep through." She took a fast breath. "Besides, I'm feeling full. It's time."

Quist's gaze fell to her breasts. He didn't say a word, just looked, but Lily felt an intense tingling warring with that sense of fullness. This tingling went deeper, curling down through her body until it settled in her womb. The sensation was nothing like the contractions she used to feel when the baby nursed. This sensation was sexual and unexpected. It had been a long time since Lily had thought of herself as a sexual being.

He raised his eyes to hers for a final, hot second before turning his attention to Nicki. Very slowly and more than a little awkwardly, reversing the motions that had brought her in to his elbow, he handed her over. Lily was able to take her in her left arm without hurting the splinted wrist, while she used her right hand to unbutton her Henley-style sweater. She was about to push the wool aside, when she paused. Her bra was already undone, since she hadn't been able to do it up with one hand after the last feeding, and pushing aside the wool meant baring her breast. Quist had seen it before, but that had been when she'd been cold and exhausted and hurting. She hadn't been thinking about him then.

She was now. She was thinking about the heat in his eyes and the heat inside her. She was thinking that it was both inappropriate and frightening, and that the smartest thing would be to turn away while she nursed. But when she started to do that, he said, "Don't. Let me watch."

His voice was low and smoky, a caress and a plea, and she couldn't say no. After all he'd done, she couldn't deny him this. Or so she told herself as she gently eased back the wool, tucked it outside her breast and brought Nicki to her nipple. But there was more. Though she kept her eyes on the baby, she could feel Quist's eyes on her. She could feel the heat. Yes, it was inappropriate and frightening. But it felt good.

Quist wasn't so sure. He was aroused—the pressure behind the placket of his fly was fierce—and he didn't know where it had come from. One minute he'd been holding the baby, thinking totally innocent thoughts, and the next he'd looked up to find Lily looking at him in a way that had turned him on.

He didn't know what was so arousing about her. He liked his women tall and shapely, with long, thick, wavy hair that could toy with a breast before he'd even put his fingers there. Lily wasn't like that at all. She was small and slender. Her hair just grazed her shoulders. Granted, her breasts were large, but that was because they were filled with milk, and because of that, he reasoned, they shouldn't turn him on.

So what was it? He supposed it was lots of things, and he supposed it had been building for a while. Nursing or not, a breast was a breast, and he was definitely a breast man. He guessed he had felt something the first time he'd seen Lily's. He knew he'd felt something when he'd helped her out of her jeans, when he'd seen the shapeliness of her legs, the softness of her skin, the curvature of her stomach. She'd been embarrassed by that, but he'd thought it sexy as hell.

And then she'd looked at him as if she found him attractive, when he'd counted on her not wanting him. He'd counted on her nixing anything before it started. He'd counted on her being the ice water to cool his fire.

Maybe it was an aberration. Maybe she was thinking of someone else, like her ex-husband or that brother-in-law she'd mentioned. No, not one of those two, he decided, but maybe someone else. He knew she was headed for Quebec to start a new life, and he knew she was alone. Still, maybe there was an old love in Quebec, someone she was planning to see, someone she'd been thinking about when she'd looked at him that way.

The thought angered him, but then, he was easy to anger when he was aroused without hope of relief. He was still aroused. *Why didn't the damn thing go down?*

It didn't go down, he told himself, because he'd asked her to let him watch her nurse, and a strangely erotic sight it was. His gaze drifted from her bare breast to her bent head to the slender fingers that, over and over, smoothed the baby's fine hair. Yes, it kept him aroused, but there was also a peace to the scene that held him there. Lily was nurturing her child as women had nurtured children since the start of time. She was loving that child in unspoken ways, and the feeling that emerged was one of serene beauty.

Quist watched with growing envy. The one thing he'd missed in life had been the kind of relationship that was so close as to be beautiful. Lily had it. Nicki would grow, and perhaps mother and daughter would have their differences, but at the moment they had something precious.

Aware that his body had finally begun to relax, he got up and added wood to the stove, then sank into the chair to watch it burn while he thought about relationships and what made them the way they were. When he saw Lily take Nicki from her breast, he found himself sitting forward and quietly asking, "Need help?"

But she easily shifted the baby to her shoulder. "I'm okay."

"Does the wrist hurt?"

"It aches, but it's better than it was. The splint helps."

Quist sat back again, this time propping his jaw on a fist. He thought back to the start of the time they'd spent together, when he'd been able to chalk Lily off as just another troublesome female and ignore her. That time had passed. He didn't think he'd ever be indifferent to her again. Even now, when his body was finally under control, he'd leaned forward and asked for more. Either he was a masochist, or Lily sparked something in him that no other woman ever had. He wasn't sure he wanted to know which it was, but in either case, he knew he couldn't sit by and watch her struggle. Time enough for struggling once they were back in civilization and went their separate ways.

Prompted by the thought, he went to the window, pulled back a shutter and peered outside. It was too dark to see much, but the low light leaking from inside the cabin revealed snow sweeping past the pane. He couldn't detect the slightest letup of the howling wind. It made him nervous to think about how much more snow had accumulated since he'd been out last.

"What time is it?" Lily called softly.

"Four-fifteen."

"No improvement?"

"Nope." He returned to his chair and sat there until Nicki was done. When Lily laid her on the mattress, he came forward. "What can I do?"

She reached for the zipper of the sleeper and began working it down, jerk by jerk, with one hand. "Uh, I don't think you want to do this."

Pushing her hand aside, he had the zipper down in a minute. Then he sat back on his heels. "What next?"

"Her legs. You have to take them out of the sleeper."

He managed that a little more slowly, gingerly holding her legs with his thumb and forefinger. Remembering what Lily had done the last time, he unsnapped the bottom of the jumpsuit, then pulled the terry cloth until first one, then the other of Nicki's feet popped free. Lily lifted both feet in one hand.

"Push the stretchsuit out of the way."

He did that. Again remembering, he carefully tore each of the diaper tapes. Then he sat on his heels and tucked his hands into the back of his jeans. He couldn't have said, "This part's yours," any louder.

PLAY
HARLEQUIN'S

LUCKY HEARTS
GAME

AND YOU COULD GET

- ★ **FREE BOOKS**
- ★ **A FREE BRACELET WATCH**
- ★ **A FREE SURPRISE GIFT**
- ★ **AND MUCH MORE**

TURN THE PAGE AND
DEAL YOURSELF IN

PLAY "LUCKY HEARTS" AND YOU COULD GET...

★ Exciting Harlequin Temptation® novels—FREE
★ A bracelet watch—FREE
★ A surprise mystery gift that will delight you—FREE

THEN CONTINUE YOUR LUCKY STREAK WITH A SWEETHEART OF A DEAL

When you return the postcard on the opposite page, we'll send you the books and gifts you qualify for, absolutely free! Then, you'll get 4 new Harlequin Temptation® novels every month, delivered right to your door months before they're available in stores. If you decide to keep them, you'll pay only $2.39* per book—that's 26 cents below the cover price and there is no extra charge for postage and handling! You can cancel at any time by marking "cancel" on your statement or returning a shipment to us at our cost.

★ Free Newsletter!

You'll get a free newsletter—an insider's look at our most popular authors and their upcoming novels.

★ Special Extras—Free!

When you subscribe to the Harlequin Reader Service®, you'll also get additional free gifts from time to time as a token of our appreciation for being a home subscriber.

*Terms and prices subject to change without notice.
Sales tax applicable in NY and Iowa.
© 1989 HARLEQUIN ENTERPRISES LIMITED

FREE BRACELET WATCH
You'll love your elegant bracelet watch—this classic LCD Quartz Watch is a perfect expression of your style and good taste—and it's yours FREE as an added thanks for giving our Reader Service a try!

HARLEQUIN'S

With a coin — scratch off the silver card and check below to see how many gifts you get.

YES! I have scratched off the silver card. Please send me all the books and gifts for which I qualify. I understand that I am under no obligation to purchase any books, as explained on the opposite page.

142 CIH MDVU (U-H-T-12/89)

NAME

ADDRESS   APT.

CITY   STATE   ZIP

Twenty-one gets you 4 free books, a free bracelet watch and mystery gift

Twenty gets you 4 free books and a free bracelet watch

Nineteen gets you 4 free books

Eighteen gets you 2 free books

PRINTED IN U.S.A.

Terms and prices subject to change. All orders subject to approval. Offer limited to one per household and not valid to current Harlequin Temptation® subscribers.
© 1989 HARLEQUIN ENTERPRISES LIMITED

DETACH AND MAIL CARD TODAY

HARLEQUIN "NO RISK" GUARANTEE

★ You're not required to buy a single book—ever!
★ As a subscriber, you must be completely satisfied or you may cancel at any time by marking "cancel" on your statement or returning a shipment of books at our cost.
★ The free books and gifts you receive from this LUCKY HEARTS offer remain yours to keep—in any case.

If offer card is missing, write to:
Harlequin Reader Service, 901 Fuhrmann Blvd., P.O. Box 1867, Buffalo, NY 14269-1867

DETACH AND MAIL CARD TODAY

BUSINESS REPLY CARD

First Class   Permit No. 717   Buffalo, NY

Postage will be paid by addressee

HARLEQUIN READER SERVICE
901 FUHRMANN BLVD
PO BOX 1867
BUFFALO NY 14240-9952

NO POSTAGE
NECESSARY
IF MAILED
IN THE
UNITED STATES

Lily didn't complain. She was impressed that he'd done so much. As quickly as possible, given the handicap of her wrist, she did her part. When she reached for a clean diaper, he came forward again to help, and though he did things more slowly than she might have if she'd had two hands, he worked faster than she could with one.

When Nicki was back in her drawer with the blankets pulled up around her, he went for the second mattress and put it foot-to-foot with the first.

Lily was vaguely disappointed. She'd enjoyed the warmth of Quist's body. But separate beds were the wisest thing, she knew. Vividly she remembered the heat that had simmered between them, and though it had cooled to a comfortable level, she knew it could rise again. Separate beds were definitely the wisest thing.

Quist turned down the hurricane lamp this time, leaving the cabin lit only by the golden glow from the stove. With the pain in her wrist nowhere near as sharp as it had been, Lily fell quickly to sleep.

As though sensing her mother's need to rest, Nicki slept for a full five hours. It was after nine-thirty in the morning when her small cries woke Lily from a deep sleep.

She yawned, then stretched, and the first thing she thought of was not her daughter, but a delightful warmth by her feet. It was a minute before she realized that those feet were entwined with Quist's. For a minute they remained that way. She could hear the storm raging outside, and the warmth inside felt so good that she didn't want to lose it.

But Nicki wanted attention. Reluctantly Lily sat up, only to have Quist wave her back down. "I'll get her," he murmured in a groggy way that was offset by the speed with which he was on his feet. He lifted the baby a little less awkwardly this time, and when she immediately stopped crying, he scowled at her. "I thought you were hungry."

"She just wanted to get up," Lily explained, rubbing sleep from her eyes. "She's probably hungry, too, but the first priority is recognition."

Quist went on scowling at Nicki. "They learn fast."

Lily considered that as she came fully awake. "We teach them. First children, especially. From the start, we come to them when they cry, so they start crying when they want us to come. Some mothers have the demands of other children or a husband or a job, so they don't do it as much. Me, I only have Lily. I've spoiled her, I guess."

"She doesn't have any grandparents?"

"My parents are dead, and if Jarrod's know she exists, they don't care. It's just as well, I suppose. If they wanted to see her, I'd have to take her back to Hartford to visit, and I don't want to do that."

The hardening of her voice was subtle, but Quist caught it. He knew that her marriage had ended badly. As odd as the time seemed now, he wanted to know more. "Was it bad all the way through?"

Disentangling herself from the blanket, Lily pushed it back and got up. "Not really." She went to her bag, took out a brush and worked it through her hair.

"What does that mean?"

She sighed. The last thing she wanted to discuss, especially two minutes after she'd woken up, was her marriage. But she couldn't be angry with Quist. He was being so helpful, and he was only curious. "It means that while I was living through it, I thought it was okay. It's only afterward that I look back and know differently." Returning the hairbrush to her bag, she looked longingly at the clothes she'd brought. She wanted to bathe in a bad way and, even more, to put on fresh things. But that would have to wait.

Coming back to Quist, she saw that Nicki was perfectly happy. Lily wasn't quite sure why, since he was holding her as if she was a sack of potatoes, albeit a valuable one, but she guessed that the novelty of his features intrigued her. Funny, his darkness hadn't made her cry. But then, she was too young to put a symbolic meaning to dark and light. Or maybe she was too smart.

"You have a way with her, Quist."

He grunted. "She'd be staring at me even if I was a side of beef."

"No. She doesn't like sides of beef. I tried that in the supermarket once. She screamed. Actually, it wasn't a side of beef. It was a steak that I put into the carrier with her. Something about it frightened her. You're much bigger, but she's not frightened." She paused to look up at him. "Will you hold her a minute longer? Since she's quiet, I can try to get some breakfast going. She may not be starved, but I am."

So was Quist. "There aren't any eggs."

"I didn't expect there would be."

"Or bacon or sausage."

So he was an egg and bacon man, she mused, crossing to study the kitchen shelves. Actually, she was an egg and bacon woman, but she hadn't expected to find either of those, and she wasn't complaining. Yesterday's fear of starvation was too fresh in her mind.

She lifted a few lids and peered inside, then bent down to scan the contents of a lower shelf. "Quist?"

"Yes?"

He was directly behind her. She shot up straight, then went red. "Sorry."

He noticed the color on her cheeks and realized that she looked better. The shadows under her eyes had faded. She didn't look as frightened or as helpless, though there was still a question in her eye. For a split second, he entertained the notion that the question had to do with sex. Then he forced himself to think sanely. "You started to ask something."

It was a split second before she remembered what it was. "The weather. We're not going anywhere today, are we?"

"Not unless the wind suddenly dies and the snow stops within the next half hour."

"Why in the next half hour?"

"Because when I go out, it's got to be first thing in the morning. It may take me a while to reach help, then a while to get it back here, and I want to be back by nightfall."

She wanted to ask why, but that seemed like pushing a good thing too far. Still she was touched. He was an incredibly kind man. For that, she decided, he deserved the best breakfast she could invent.

Actually, she didn't have to invent a thing, since pancakes had been breakfast fare for generations. She supposed lacing them with peanut butter was a novelty, and she doubted she'd want to enter the recipe in the bake-off, but the end result was edible and nourishing.

Quist loved it. He was great at opening cans and cooking up frozen dinners and reheating leftovers, and he could fry a mean egg and grill a rasher of bacon just right, but he wasn't one to put together a meal from scratch. He was surprised that Lily had done it. He hadn't expected she'd be much of a cook, but she'd managed well, even with a bum hand. Nicki had started to cry just as the first batch of pancakes were done, so he'd taken over with the spatula, but that was okay. It wasn't like Lily had left the kitchen in the middle of things to polish her toenails. He could wield a spatula. And the pancakes were great.

With Nicki fed and changed, Lily laid her on the table and sat down for her own breakfast. Nursing a second cup of cocoa, Quist watched her eat. Though she talked softly to Nicki from time to time, she seemed otherwise content with the silence. He wondered whether she'd become as used to solitude as he had, or whether she'd always been that way. He didn't ask, though. The silence was too comfortable just then.

When she'd finished, Lily looked at him and smiled. Seconds later, she shifted her gaze to the window and the smile faded. "This is unreal," she murmured.

He'd liked her smile. It had done things to him, and he was sorry it was gone. But he knew what she meant. Unreal was one word for their situation; bizarre was another. "Uh-huh." He saw her looking down at her splinted wrist. "How does it feel?"

She hesitated before answering, "Okay."

"Does that mean better?"

She nodded. It still ached, but the ache was more dull than acute. One part of her wanted to think that it wasn't broken, after all. The other part recalled the pain she'd felt when Quist had manipulated it the night before. No sprain felt like that.

"I should have known it was broken."

"You didn't want it to be."

"No, but I should have known. I always manage to do things like that."

"You didn't do it on purpose."

She sighed, still looking down. "I didn't purposely come down with chicken pox the night before I was to play Dorothy in my seventh grade class's production of 'The Wizard of Oz,' either. Or break out with poison ivy the day before my high school prom. Or have my rental car stolen with all my things inside when I was driving to college to start my sophomore year." She frowned, feeling the pain inside her head rather than at her wrist. "This couldn't have happened at a worse time." Her voice dropped to a whisper. "I have so many things to do."

"So you'll just do them slower."

She shrugged and got up from the table with the dishes. She didn't want to think about it. It was too discouraging. So many things to do, simple but important things that were going to be twice as difficult for her now. It wasn't fair.

Quist carried a pot of hot water to the sink. "I'll do them this time."

"*I'll* do them," she insisted. Swishing the dishes around in soapy water was one of the few things she could do single-handedly, and while she regretted her snappish tone, she had to be assertive. Quist was doing far too much.

Preoccupied wondering how she was going to do all those other things, she finished the dishes without another thought to Quist. When she was done and turned, though, she went very still.

He was shaving. Sitting at the table with his back to her, he was stripped to the waist. A small mirror was propped against the worn leather shaving kit. A small pan of hot water stood before that. He was stroking the blade up his neck, making neat, consecutive furrows in the shaving cream.

But it wasn't his neck to which her eyes were drawn, so much as his back. It was a broad expanse of skin stretched over tight muscles that moved with each stroke. She'd already guessed him to be fit. She'd already guessed at his tapering shape. She hadn't guessed at the raw power of his body, or at the powerful effect seeing it bare would have on her.

Her heart began to pound as she stood there, unable to take her eyes away. She noted the way spikes of dark hair fell over his nape when he tipped up his chin, the way the muscles of his shoulder bunched when he reached the apex of each stroke, the way tufts of dark hair shadowed his armpits. She saw a pale scar, jagged but old, lying somewhere in the vicinity of his waist, but it was hard to tell just where that waist was, since his jeans rode low on his hips. She traced his spine up to his shoulders, then dropped her gaze again until it hit his jeans. But her mind didn't stop at denim. It went on to the small of his back, then stole around to his front to see what was there.

Covering her eyes with her arm, she tried to get hold of herself. The baby would help, she decided, so she went to the table, leaned over Nicki, cooed to her for a minute and lifted her. Then, with the baby held tightly in her arms, her eyes went to Quist.

His chest was breathtaking, his muscles well-defined without being overdeveloped. He wasn't heavily haired, but what there was created a soft pelt that was broad and tapering, a visual echo of the shape of his body. His nipples were small and dark brown. He had a beauty mark just below the right one and a scar several inches below that.

"Lily."

She raised her eyes to find that he'd stopped shaving.

"What are you doing?" he asked in a low voice.

She tried to moisten her lips, but the inside of her mouth was dry. Her throat must have been, too, because her voice came out sounding parched. "Holding Nicki."

"That's not what I mean."

She swallowed. "I'm thinking that maybe I could bathe her when you're done."

His eyes glittered, daring her to tell him the truth.

"Well, you were just sitting there," she burst out. "I mean, I was doing the dishes and suddenly turned around and there you were with your shirt off. What did you expect me to do?"

"I didn't expect you'd stare that way," he said very quietly. "You've seen a man with his shirt off before."

"I know."

"You've seen a man shave before."

"Yes, but—"

"Is it just that it's been a long time, that you're hungry?"

"I'm not!" she cried. "I just had a baby. The *last* thing on my mind is sex."

He paused before saying, still in that same very quiet voice that was more pointed than a shout and every bit as dangerous, "It was there just now."

"And it's your fault!" She dropped her voice to mutter, "Sitting there like that, with a chest like yours," then raised her voice again, "What do you expect?" Turning on her heel, she stomped off to the front of the cabin and glared at her open bag.

"I expect," Quist said from directly behind her, "that you'll use a little self-control. I'm a man. You can't count on me for it."

"You don't need it. I'm not the one who's sexy."

"Who told you that?"

"I know it. I'm not gorgeous to begin with, and now that I've got a baby, I'm about as attractive to a man as a piece of mush."

His voice was closer. "I wouldn't say that."

"You would if you weren't shut up in this tiny place with me."

"But I am shut up in here with you, and it doesn't help things when you look at me the way you just did."

She knew that he was directly behind her. The heat of his body reached out to her, joining with the images of his bareness in her mind to play havoc with her insides. To blot out those images, she buried her face against Nicki's head, but the name she whispered was Quist's.

The heat came even closer then, a line of fire touching her from her shoulders to the backs of her knees. "I want you, Lily."

She shook her head, but couldn't utter a word.

Lowering his head over hers, he put his lips to her temple. The rest of his body did a similar kind of nuzzling. "You're not my type, still I want you. Can you feel it?"

A little frantic, she nodded.

"Then I would suggest," he said slowly and with deliberation, "that you make a point not to encourage me. If you let on that the feeling is mutual, I can't promise I won't take you." The last was said against her neck and was punctuated by a slow, suckling kiss that made Lily feel faint. But just when she needed him most, he stepped back. Furious in her frustration, she put a hand to the spot he'd kissed and whirled on him. "You gave me a hickey."

"Not this time," he said. More softly, he promised, "Next time," and before she could think of an appropriate comeback, he was sauntering back to the table.

Senses in an uproar, she collapsed onto the bare springs of the cot, held Nicki close and rocked back and forth. The squeaking of the springs joined with the sounds of the storm to emphasize the absurdity of the situation, as did a certain scent that was coming to her. It wasn't exactly the musky, male scent that had already etched itself on her brain, but a more immediate scent.

Touching her temple, she brought her hand down with traces of shaving cream. She found them on her neck, too, and would have screamed if it would have done any good. But self-control was what she needed, certainly not another confrontation with Quist. She was attracted to him. Okay, she was. But she'd get past it. It was nothing more than another hurdle to be cleared.

Taking several deep breaths, she sat up straight and turned her attention to Nicki.

Quist finished shaving and bathed himself as best he could with the water that remained and one of the towels he'd taken from the drawer. When he was done, he went for a clean shirt. That meant passing close by Lily, but she seemed determined not to look. He looked at her, though, as he buttoned the clean shirt, and when he was done, he said, "Do you want to bathe the kid?"

"Yes."

Pulling his boots on, he went outside to refill the largest pot with snow. He set the whole thing on top of the stove to melt. The process gave Lily plenty of time to undress Nicki, which she did on a blanket directly in front of the woodstove, where it was comfortably warm. By the time the water was hot, she was ready to go.

Quist watched. He told himself that he wanted to make sure Lily didn't injure her hand, but there was a definite curiosity factor involved. He wanted to see what she was going to do and how. He also wanted to see her doing it, because he liked watching her care for Nicki. It brought out the serenity factor, and though it reminded him of everything he missed, and in that sense was painful, he was helplessly drawn to it.

That serenity factor wasn't as strong, now, though, as it had been at other times, and Quist could see why. Splinted and awkward, Lily's wrist kept interfering with what she was trying to do. She shifted, lifting Nicki different ways, doing the best with what she had, but it clearly wasn't enough to satisfy her. Though she continued to talk softly and gently to the baby, her features grew tense, reflecting her frustration.

By the time she'd wrapped a wet and naked Nicki in a towel, she was near tears. That was when he came forward. "Damn it, won't you ever ask for help?"

She sat back on her heels, put her hands on her hips and, looking at the baby, said stonily, "I don't want help."

"Maybe not, but it'd be a hell of a lot easier on both of us if you admitted you could use it."

"I have to do this myself."

"Why?"

"Nicki's my responsibility."

"Yeah, but I'm sitting here doing nothing. Why not make use of me?"

She looked him in the eye. "Because that puts us close. Better we shouldn't be close."

He ran a hand through his hair, which had already dried from the dunking he'd given it and fell right back over his brow. "Better you should get this done. It's worse watching you."

Lily wasn't sure exactly what that meant, but she didn't have time to ask before he was leaning over to pat the baby dry. While Lily took care of the delicate parts, he helped with the others, and Nicki was happy enough with the dual attention to kick and coo and smile. By the time he handed her over, she was dressed in a pretty pink stretchsuit, her hair was brushed and her cheeks had the polish of early apples. Closing her eyes, Lily breathed deeply of that sweet baby smell she adored, and smiled. When Nicki yawned, she kissed her tiny, button nose and held her for several more minutes, then neatened the drawer and put her in for a nap.

Quist's voice came from the world behind her. "Are you next?" He had a clean towel in his hand. Rising, she took it. He lowered his voice. "Want me to help?"

"Of course not," she whispered, eyes wide and glued to his.

"Can you manage by yourself?" The intimacy of his tone was matched by his look.

"Yes," she said in the wisp of breath he left her. She was able to breathe more deeply only when he turned away.

Disposing of the water she'd used for the baby, he refilled the smaller pot with hot water and set it on the table. When he looked at her again, his eyes were dark and sensual. "If I were a martyr, I'd offer to go out and wander around in the storm for fifteen minutes, but I'm no martyr." He turned one of the Adirondack chairs so that it faced the front of the cabin, dropped into it and said, "I won't watch."

Lily swallowed and stood stock-still. The air was pregnant with a silence that not even the storm could fill.

"Well?" he prompted without turning. "You'd better get to it. Like I said, I'm no martyr. I won't sit here forever."

That brought her to life. Taking clean clothes and a small bottle of lotion from her bag, she went to the table. For another minute she looked at Quist; only his dark hair and navy sweater were visible through the slats of the chair. Realizing that she had no choice but to trust him, she turned around, eased the sweater over her head, then over the wrist with the splint, and began to wash.

Quist didn't look once. He wanted to, and several times he came close—mainly because he hoped that the real thing would be less impressive than his imagination—but he stayed true to his word. His mind was so preoccupied thinking about what she'd be like naked, though, that he was unprepared when she materialized by his side fully clothed, looking fresh and combed and even more sweet-smelling than the baby. She wasn't on a pleasure mission, though.

"I think this needs tightening," she said quietly, cradling the splinted wrist in the good one. She looked a little pale.

"It hurts?"

She nodded.

Urging her down in front of him, he took the wrist onto his thigh and, one by one, released and retied the strips of cloth that held it tight. When he'd finished, he took the fingers extending from the splint and very gently moved them.

"Hurt?"

"A little."

"But not as much as yesterday?"

"No."

"That's good." With the splint braced on his thigh, he held her fingers in his palm, traced their slenderness with his thumb. "You don't wear a ring."

She looked at her hand, saw what his thumb was doing, found it soothing. "I'm divorced."

"Did you get the divorce, or did he?"

"He did. He wanted it fast."

"What was the rush?"

"His girlfriend was pregnant."

"So were you."

She raised her eyes. "So?"

"So his loyalties were misplaced. You were his wife. He should have stayed with you until you'd had the baby."

"I didn't want that any more than he did," she said, and he saw the pride that lifted her chin.

"But it must have been hard, being alone through all that."

"It would have been worse if we'd been together. Everything would have been right there—the anger, the resentment, the distrust. I'd have been a nervous wreck, and Nicki would have suffered." She shook her head. "Better being alone than living with that."

He could understand the rationale. It was one he'd adhered to most of his life. "Did you ever see him after that?"

"Not if I could help it."

"What about your brother-in-law?"

Her features tightened. "What about him?"

"Did he offer to help?"

She looked back at her hand in time to see her fingers curving around his. "Did he offer to help? I guess you could call it that." She took a shaky breath. "He offered to take credit for Nicki in exchange for my... servicing him."

At thought of the service, Quist swore softly. At thought of Nicki, he said, "Take credit for her? But she already had a father."

"That's right. Michael threatened to say that he'd had an affair with me, that Jarrod wasn't her father at all. The only way I could keep him from doing that, he said, was to sleep with him."

"Did he want you that much?"

"Me?" She gave a brittle laugh. "He didn't want me. He wanted to sock one to Jarrod. They'd been rivals all their lives. He thought he could take advantage of the way I was feeling to get back at his brother. It would have given him great pleasure to let Jarrod think he'd been making it with his wife."

Quist made a face. "What kind of sickness is that?"

"Sickness?" She raised sad eyes to his. "You don't know the half. When I refused him, he got ugly."

"Ugly? Like how?"

"Yelling. Name-calling. Violent, I guess."

"You guess?"

"He started throwing things. If it hadn't been for my next door neighbor knocking on the door, I'm not sure what I'd have done."

Quist was quiet, staring into her eyes for a long time. At last, very quietly, he asked, "When was all this?"

Taking her hand back into her lap, she stood. "Three days ago." She went to the window, wrapped her arms around herself and stared out at the gusting snow.

It was easy enough to figure out. "So you ran."

Hurt in her eyes, she whirled around. "I had to. I couldn't stay there, not living under that kind of threat, *especially* not with Nicki's welfare to consider." Her eyes followed him, barely aware that he'd come out of his seat. "You don't know these people, Quist. They have power and money, and they have no qualms about using either or both when it suits their purposes." Her eyes rose as he approached. "Michael would have kept after me, maybe threatened something else, and Jarrod might have lashed back, but I'd be the one hurt. Me, and Nicki. So why should I stay in Hartford? I stayed there during my pregnancy because my doctor was there and a few friends, but all along I knew that I'd be leaving. There was no future for me there. Thanks to Michael, I made the move sooner, that's all."

Feeling the need to comfort, Quist lightly stroked her arms. "What's in Quebec?"

"I'll find out soon."

"Do you know anyone there?"

She shook her head. "It's supposed to be a nice place, and if I don't like it, I'll move on. I'm a legal secretary, and a good one. I can work anywhere there are lawyers."

"What about Nicki?"

She swallowed hard. "I'll find someone to look after her while I work."

"Is that what you want?"

"It's not what I want at all," she cried, "but what choice do I have? I'm not like Jarrod or his family. I don't have contacts in scads of cities. My parents were quiet, private people who struggled to pay the bills until the day they died." She caught in a breath and added, "I thought I'd escaped that."

"Is that why you married him?" Quist asked, but even before the words were out she was shaking her head.

"I thought I loved him. I thought he loved me. I thought we were a solid couple, because I was a foil for his flamboyance. I calmed him down, so he said. I thought it was true. I thought that I was sensitive enough to understand his mood swings and smart enough to anticipate his needs. I thought that the differences in our backgrounds didn't matter and that his parents would come around in time. I thought we'd have a house and a car and kids and a dog. I thought—I thought we could have it all." She sucked in a breath and held it for a shaky second before releasing it in a ragged whoosh. "I thought wrong."

Tears shimmered on her lower lids, underlining the anguish in her eyes. Quist felt the pain of that anguish, but before he could act on it, she said in a soulful whisper, "All I wanted...all I wanted was to be a good wife. I didn't want personal recognition. I didn't want a career. I didn't even want to be named to the board of one of the corporate subsidiaries. All I wanted was to keep house, to be a good wife and a good mother. Was that so awful?"

He drew her close and wrapped her in his arms. She didn't cry. But her body trembled as it sank into his, and her arm stole around his waist and clung.

She drank in his strength without thought as to why she shouldn't. She needed him just then, needed him to hold her, to tell her she was worth holding. She'd been alone for too long with her fears and her worries. She needed to feel that she had a friend.

She'd never had one quite like this, though—one whose body could protect and comfort and at the same time excite. She'd never had one who made her feel delicate, while he held her so tight, or one who felt so vibrant or smelled so good in such an unadorned way.

So many sensations, so many emotions. She felt dazed when he drew back and looked down into her face. His own was as dark as always, but his eyes were alive, relaying the message of his body. Her lips softened. Her pulse raced. She wasn't so dazed that she didn't know what was happening when he lowered his head—nor was she so dazed that she didn't know that, right then, she wanted his kiss more than anything else in the world.

6

His MOUTH touched hers. It was a tentative touch, a brief sampling that quickly called for another. The second, then the third were the same, gentle enough to be nonthreatening, firm enough to offer the comfort for which they had been originally intended.

At least Quist told himself he was offering comfort, but the question was to whom, and the issue was drawing the line between comfort and desire. He knew he was doing something to Lily, because her lips softened beneath his and her body went pliant, losing the tension he'd felt when she'd been telling her story and he'd first touched her. And he knew that he felt better with her in his arms, tasting her mouth, breathing in her sweet woman's scent. But his body wasn't pliant; it was growing harder by the minute. So, was desire a comfort? That depended on where it led, he supposed.

But supposition had its place, and it wasn't there, at that moment in time. Sensation was taking over, driving him to deepen the kiss. His tongue outlined her lips, first outside, then inside. When it met resistance at her teeth, he returned to a more innocent caress, and soon, with a tiny sigh of surrender, she asked him in.

He didn't wait to be asked twice. With gentle force, his tongue swept the hidden depths of her mouth. He breathed her breath and gave his own in return, and in so doing, possessed her in ways that went far beyond a kiss.

She was lost, unaware of anything but Quist. The storm might well not have been, nor the cabin, nor Nicki. Quist filled her senses to overflowing—the strength of his body as he held her, the gentleness of his touch, the fire he sparked. He made her forget everything else, and she needed that. He made her feel feminine, and she needed that, too. But he gave her a sense of hope, and that was what she needed most of all.

It was also, in the end, what made her draw back. Her body was heated and trembling, arching into his with a primal ache, yet she made a small sound and tore her mouth away. She didn't release her hold of his waist; she couldn't quite let go of everything at once, and besides, she didn't trust her legs to support her. But she laid her head on his chest and closed her eyes in an attempt to corral her senses into some kind of order.

Quist kept one arm around her back. He cupped her head with his free hand and held it close while he raised his own high and dragged in labored breaths in an attempt to regain firm footing on the ground. Only when he felt he'd done that did he lower his head.

"Lily?"

Her voice was muffled against his sweater. "I'm okay."

"I won't apologize for that."

"I don't want you to." She paused, then asked very cautiously, "Was it me?"

He didn't know what she meant. "You?"

"Me. As opposed to someone else."

"There's no one else here."

"In your life."

"What are you talking about?"

She let out a small, muffled sigh. "Has it been a long time since you've been with a woman?"

"It's been a while."

"Oh."

She sounded disappointed, which surprised him. He'd have thought she'd be pleased. Bemused, he cupped her head with both hands and turned her face up. Her cheeks were flushed, her eyes large and gray. He would have kissed them closed if he hadn't been distracted by her reaction. "What in the devil's going through your mind?"

"You're horny."

That much was obvious, since his erection was pressing against his jeans, which were in turn pressing against hers. "A man can't hide things like a woman can."

"But you're horny because you haven't had a woman in a long time. So it wasn't me. It was my being a woman. That's all."

He was beginning to get her drift. She was feeling insecure, and based on what she'd said about her marriage, he could understand why. She was also distrustful of men, but she'd told him that at the start. He hadn't imagined then that it would bother him so much.

Tightening his hold of her head, he said with some force, "I see women. I see them all the time. I may be a goddamned cowboy, but it's not like I'm out on the range for six months at a time. I'm in town two or three times a week, and I travel farther at least once a month. So there are women. If I haven't had one for a long time, it's by choice, which means that it's also by choice if I want one now."

His eyes fell to her lips and lingered there. "You taste so damned good," he muttered under his breath. As though chagrined by the admission, he looked her in the eye and went on more sternly. "So don't ever suggest that I'd take just any woman. I'm picky. I don't make love to one while I'm thinking of another, and I don't make love *at all* unless it's to the woman I want." He stared hard at her for another minute before softening. "I've already said you turn me on. You'd better believe it."

Lily wanted to. Then again, she didn't. In fact, the more she thought about it, the more she realized that she didn't want to believe it at all. She didn't want it to be so. She didn't want to be involved that way with Quist, not when her life was in such a state of confusion.

"I need a friend," she whispered, "not a lover."

Arching a dark brow, he drawled, "That wasn't no friendly kiss you just gave me, baby."

"I didn't give you anything. I just . . . *let* you—" she gritted her teeth "—and it's Lily, not baby. I hate being called something I'm not." Pulling free of him, she moved a step back. That was all it took to put her up against the wall. To compensate, she tipped up her chin.

Quist took in the staunchness of her expression and remembered other times she'd taken similar exception to what he'd said. Suddenly he realized why. "He did that, didn't he? Your husband did that."

"Ex-husband, and yes. When I worked in the office, I was his girl. When I dated him, I was his honey. When I married him, I was his sugar. But the worst, the *worst*, was baby. That started sometime during the second year of our marriage, when the glow had worn off and the monotony set in. I told myself it was nothing more than another little term of endearment, but it always bothered me. It was short and crude and condescending. More than that, it's a cop-out. A man can call any number of women baby, or sugar or honey. It's easy. He doesn't have to remember a name, and he doesn't risk using the wrong name on the wrong woman." She took in a fast breath and her tone grew pleading. "So, please, call me Lily. Not lady, or sweetheart, or baby. Lily. Or nothing at all."

As abruptly as she finished talking, she dropped her chin and looked at the floor. Quist allowed that for just a second before he took her chin in his fingers and lifted it.

"Let's get a few things straight," he said.

"A few *more* things," she corrected.

"Okay. A few *more* things. First off," he began, dark eyes flashing, "I am not like your ex-husband. I don't use women—or if I do, they know it right from the start and agree to the terms. Second, when I use words like lady or sweetheart, I do it to express something I'm feeling at that moment, whether it's anger or affection. I don't do it to avoid calling one woman by another's name. I don't have to. Because—point number three—I believe in monogamy. I have never been involved with more than one woman at a time. One woman is about all I can handle, and if she isn't, then she's all wrong for me. And fourth," his fingers tightened on her chin, "I want *you*, not just any woman, and not just because we're marooned out here in the middle of a goddamned blizzard. There's nothing sexy about being stuck here when I'm supposed to be somewhere else, and there's nothing sexy about that bare-bones mattress on the floor over there. I'm forty years old. I've roughed it plenty. I've earned the right to creature comforts, and making love on a skinny, lumpy bed isn't one. Nor is doing it on a hardwood floor or against a drafty wall."

He paused, mesmerized by the wide-eyed look on her face. She was so innocent. It was hard to believe. "Besides," he said more quietly, even distractedly as his attention drifted to her mouth, "There's no way I could confuse you with any other woman I've known. You're different from the rest in every possible way."

Lily wanted to think that was a compliment, but she wasn't sure. "What are the others like?" she heard herself whisper.

With a sniff, he shot a glance toward the eaves. "Tall. Buxom. Curvy. Blond." He brushed the pad of his thumb on her chin. "And none of them have kids."

"Why didn't you marry one of them?"

"I'm not interested in marriage. You should have guessed that."

"Because you don't like women?" He'd been blunt about that from the first. "For a man who doesn't like women, it sounds like you've been involved with an awful lot. I'm surprised one of them didn't con you into it."

He straightened. "No one cons me into anything. And that's a vow." As though to second it, the muscle in his jaw jumped.

Lily knew what he was thinking. "It's not a vow, it's a warning, but it's unnecessary. I couldn't con you if I wanted to. I don't know how. Besides, I don't *want* to con you into anything. The only thing I want is to get my car out of that snowdrift and get back on my way to Quebec."

Curling his fingers around her neck, he said, "It'll be at least two or three days before that happens, and in the meantime..."

"In the meantime, what?" she asked, but she could tell from the look in his eyes what he was thinking.

"In the meantime, anything can happen."

"It won't."

"It almost did, right here, a minute ago."

"That was just a kiss, for God's sake."

"It was more than that, and you know it. It was a preview." He leaned closed. "You felt it deep inside, just like I did."

She shook her head.

"Yes, you did, Lily." His voice lowered. "You feel it even now." His hand came from the back of her neck. He rubbed the backs of his fingers over her throat. "And don't say you've just had a baby so you're not interested in sex, because I'm not convinced one follows the other. You may not have kissed me back, but you enjoyed what I did."

"I didn't ask for it."

"But you enjoyed it." His voice grew more intimate. "And you'd enjoy it if I touched you more." He ran the backs of his fingers down between her breasts to her middle, ignoring her gasp of surprise. "Come to think of it, having a baby is a pretty sexy thing. There's only one way to get pregnant."

Lily's heart was beating faster. "Not today. There are lots of ways today."

He was drawing light circles just above her navel. "But sperm has to meet egg and do its thing. There's something inherently sexual about that, regardless of where it takes place."

"You're playing with words," she said a bit breathlessly.

"And you're picking at straws." His hand came slowly up, fingers dragging along her sweater, creating friction and an incredible heat. "Admit it. You're feeling sexy."

"I'm not."

He caressed the side of her breast. "How about now?"

She shook her head.

He brushed her nipple. "And now?"

A tiny sound came from the back of her throat, still she shook her head.

"You're a liar," Quist whispered, but with an odd affection, as he settled his hips against hers. "Why deny it? It's no crime." Back and forth went the backs of his fingers over that tightly budded crest. His cheek was against her forehead, his voice not much more than a breath against her eyes. "I can feel it. It's hard and aching."

Lily could feel it, too, but from the inside. His touch was pulling all kinds of strings linking her breast to the center of her being. "I don't feel sexy," she managed in a husky voice. "I feel aroused. There's a difference."

He was willing to settle for aroused. God only knew he was that, himself. Breathing more roughly than he had moments before, he opened his palm and cupped her breast fully.

"Don't."

"Shh. It's okay. I won't hurt you."

Hurting her wasn't the problem, at least, not in the traditional sense. She was beginning to ache inside, wanting something she couldn't have. And his hand wasn't helping with its sweet stroking, the kneading that gave definition to her flesh. Each time he buzzed her nipple she felt a surge of heat.

"Please," she gasped.

"Please, what?"

"Stop. Please, stop."

But he didn't. He kept touching her, and she didn't so much as grab his hand, because what he was doing felt so good. She felt as though she was awakening after a long sleep, as though she was stretching and purring and coming alive in ways she'd never been before. Her breathing was shallow and fast, her forehead pressed to his cheek. She felt female all over.

Quist thought so, too. While one of his hands stroked her breast, the other was exploring things like her waist and her hips, even her thighs, and nothing he found was a disappointment. But he was, after all, a breast man. Wrapping that other arm fully around her waist to anchor her close, he slipped a hand under her sweater and, before she could protest, cupped her swollen flesh.

She gasped, then followed it with a tiny moan of helpless pleasure and mindless need. She hadn't expected the sensual onslaught. She wasn't prepared for it at all.

"Quist," she whispered, and there was a frantic edge to the sound.

He heard it. Not for a minute did he think it anything but what it was. She wasn't asking for more, though one part of her wanted it. She was asking him, one last time, to stop. She was saying that she wouldn't be able to ask him again, but that she didn't want to make love. She was frightened.

So was he, in his way. He'd had his fire stoked many a time, but never to quite the combustible level he was at now. His muscles were tight, his blood heated. He was on the verge of losing control. He had to think, had to decide whether that was what he wanted to do.

Breathing hard, memorizing the feel of her for a final greedy moment, he dragged his hand over her flesh and out from under her sweater. "This is absurd," he grumbled. "This whole thing is absurd. There shouldn't be any attraction between us."

"I know," she cried in a wobbly voice.

"We're as different as night from day."

"Yes."

"We want different things. Once we leave this cabin, we'll go our separate ways and never see each other again."

She nodded against his chest.

"So what are we doing?"

"I'm not doing anything. You're the one who's doing— and don't say that I didn't fight you, because I know I didn't, so I'm as bad as you are."

"Worse," he said. Unfulfilled desire always made him cranky. "I told you not to count on me for control, but you did it. So where does that leave us now? I'm hard and you're scared."

"Maybe you'd better let me go."

"But I like the feel of you against me."

"It's useless. It can't go anywhere."

He moved then, not far, but enough to allow for breathing space. "Can't?" It was a possibility he hadn't considered, but he eyed her in concern and considered it now. "Was there some problem when you had Nicki? Are you not completely healed or something?" She'd done pretty well going through the snow, right up until the end. It was hard to remember she'd been through childbirth such a short time before.

"I meant can't, as in won't."

But he wasn't convinced about the other. "Are you okay, Lily? If things were different, if we knew each other in normal circumstances, if you wanted to do it, could you make love?"

She was a long time answering, and then it was in a defeated voice directed at the far wall. "I should say no. That would be best for both of us. You'd know that you couldn't do it, and I'd know that I lied, so I wouldn't deserve to do it." She looked meekly up. "I haven't been to the doctor yet. I was supposed to see him next week." She hesitated for another minute, finally admitting very quietly. "But I'm fine. I know my body. It's healed."

Quist was glad for her, not so glad for him. Temptation was staring him in the face, and he didn't like it.

Crossing her arms over her waist, Lily balanced her splinted wrist in the crook of her elbow. Her face was averted. "I was only with one man before my husband, and that was long before my marriage. I'm not good at things like this."

"Neither am I," Quist said. "The other women I've been with have known the score."

Her head went lower. "I'm sorry. I wish I was more sophisticated—"

"Oh, please," he snarled, turning away with a hand at the back of his neck. "If you were more sophisticated, I probably wouldn't want you so much. Besides, wishes are pointless. They don't do us any good."

She pulled in her arms. "What will?"

"Determination." He faced her again, and his expression was as firm as his voice. "We're not making love. That's that. The attraction is skin-deep. You don't want a cowboy any more than I want a new mother. We'll be here together for another one, two, maybe three days, but after that it's over. So we're just gonna have to use a little self-control."

"You said I couldn't count on you for it."

"I'm not sure you can. I'll try. You just be sure to try double hard."

Lily put her head back against the wood and closed her eyes for a minute. She could try double hard. She was good at doing that. It seemed she'd been doing it all her life. Ah, but she was tired of the struggle.

Her eyes flew open when Quist suddenly grasped her arms and hauled her away from the wall. She was thinking that his resolve hadn't lasted long at all, when he said, "You'll freeze standing there." He dropped one hand, kept the other at her arm as he led her to the chair nearest the woodstove. When she'd settled into it, he turned the other around to face the same way and sank down. He stretched out his legs, propped his elbows on the broad wooden arms, pressing his fists together against his mouth. Seconds later he mumbled something.

Lily looked up. "Hmm?"

He dropped his fists to his lap. "You didn't feel the cold, did you?" It was more a statement than a question. No, she hadn't felt the cold, and they both knew why. "And your wrist wasn't hurting." He didn't even attempt to make that one a question. She'd been aroused. Everything in the periphery had fallen away. "It was powerful," he said a bit wistfully, keeping his eyes on the slow-burning logs.

There wasn't much Lily could add. He'd captured the feeling in two short statements and three words. Dwelling on it, though, wasn't going to help with self-control. They needed a diversion.

"Why are you headed for Quebec?" she asked. It seemed as good a diversion as any, and besides, she wanted to know.

He shot her a fast glance before looking back at the woodstove, and he was silent for a while. Finally he rubbed a finger across the bridge of his nose. "I'm looking for someone. Last I heard, she was there."

"She?" Lily felt stung.

"My half sister."

The sting eased. "Your mother's daughter?"

His nod was slow and tight. "She's in some kind of trouble. Called me two weeks ago from New York and asked if I'd come, but when I got there she'd gone to Boston, and when I got there, she'd gone to Quebec. I'm giving it this one last shot, and if she isn't in Quebec, I'm on my way." He half sang the last, the message being that he'd be on his way without regret.

"What kind of trouble is she in?"

"Man trouble. She got involved with someone who wasn't very nice. The question is whether he takes the fall alone, or whether he drags her down with him."

"What can you do?"

"Get her a good lawyer."

"She can't do that herself?"

"She's only nineteen."

"Nineteen! That's . . . surprising."

His mouth grew hard. "My mother was seventeen when she had me. She was thirty-eight when she had her. For all I know, there were others in between, but I only heard of Jennifer. I got a call from a lawyer one day saying that my mother had died and there was a daughter I was supposed to be told about. So I was told."

There was more that he wasn't saying. "You've never seen her, have you?"

"Nope."

"Were you in touch with her at all before this?"

He pursed his lips and shook his head.

She offered him a tentative smile of admiration. "Still you've come all the way across the country to help her. I think that's nice."

"Not really. I'm just satisfying my curiosity."

"It has to be more than that," she chided, still wearing that tentative smile. "If it was only curiosity, you'd have come to take a look at her long ago."

"I didn't know about her long ago. It's only been five years since my mother died."

Lily's smile faded. "Did you ever see your mother again, I mean, after she left?"

"No."

She rubbed her arm against the chill in his voice. "You never tried to find her?"

"Why would I have done that? She was the one who left. She didn't give a damn about me. Was I supposed to care what happened to her?"

"Weren't you ever curious?"

"I had enough to keep me busy so I didn't have to think of it."

"But she was your mother."

"An accident of birth."

Lily glanced toward the drawer in which Nicki was napping, and it occurred to her that one day her daughter would say the same thing about Jarrod. And Lily would do nothing to discourage it. Lord knew, *she* didn't want contact with Jarrod. "But Nicki may be curious," she told herself. Realizing that she'd spoken aloud, she sent Quist a self-conscious look. "I was thinking about Nicki and her father."

"Obviously."

"I'm not sure how I'll handle it."

"When she asks about her father?"

Lily nodded. "It's not an immediate problem. While she's little, she'll accept the answers I give her. But if she decides she wants to see him when she's older, I don't know."

"You can't forbid it."

"I don't want her hurt. What if she pops up on his doorstep and he slams the door in her face? Can you imagine what she'd feel?"

"I can imagine," he said, and Lily realized that he, more than most, could imagine, indeed.

"God, I hope that never happens," she whispered, nervously fiddling with the ragged ends of the cloth strips binding her splint.

"What if he comes looking for her one day?"

Her eyes flew up. "He has no right."

"He has every right. He's her father."

But Lily was shaking her head. "As far as I'm concerned, he surrendered his rights where Nicki's concerned the day he walked out on us."

"A court would say differently."

"Whose side are you on?" she cried.

"I'm not taking sides. I'm just being realistic."

Calming herself a little, she realized that he was right. Only he didn't know the facts. "I have papers. Jarrod signed them. He agreed to leave us alone."

Quist considered that. "In exchange for what?"

She had to hand it to him; he was quick. And it seemed silly, since she'd already told him so much, not to tell the rest. "A lump-sum settlement that was below what I might have gotten if I'd wanted to fight him. Jarrod's family is powerful. They never accepted me as one of them, and I could imagine all kinds of nasty things happening if they decided they wanted part of Nicki. I won't have her used that way. I was willing to give up the money for a certain peace of mind."

"So now you have to work."

"I don't have to. The settlement was still a good one. But I want to put it away for Nicki—for education, maybe travel or a home when she's grown." She rubbed her arm. "I don't want that money for myself. I'd rather work."

Quist had to admire her for that, but his thoughts were straying. He was remembering what it was like growing up with one parent and no siblings. "She'll be lonely."

"Maybe not. I'll be there most of the time. And if I meet the right man, I'll remarry and have more kids."

He eyed her warily. "Is that what you want?"

She had no qualms about saying, "Yes," and looking him in the eye. "I meant it when I said I didn't want a career. I can work, and I'll happily do it as long as I have to, but I'm not ambitious that way. I want a home and a family. I want to bake bread and drive car pools and barbecue hotdogs on Sunday afternoons. That's all I've ever really wanted."

When she'd said it before, it had been in the context of her marriage to Jarrod. He hadn't given it much thought then. Now he did. "You're a throwback. Women aren't wanting to do things like that nowadays. They want to be out having fun, making money, putting men in their places, or trying to."

"Not me," she said simply. Resting her head against the back of the chair, she closed her eyes.

Quist stared at her, waiting for her to look at him and tell him how cynical he was, or that he knew the wrong women. The fact that she didn't move, didn't speak, didn't even open her eyes somehow gave greater credence to her claim. If she was a throwback to women of an earlier age, she was making no apologies for it.

He almost envied the man she married, and she would marry, he knew. She wasn't meant to be a loner. She'd make some man a good wife. She was nice to be with, eager to please, willing to do her share of the work. She was bright and attractive. And sexy. He looked at the way her sweater fell loosely over her breasts and remembered how that flesh had felt in his hands. Too quickly he felt a stirring in his loins.

Fortunately Nicki woke up just then, and he was almost relieved. He needed something to take his mind off Lily's body. Picking the baby up, carrying her to Lily, helping change her diapers were the kinds of things that—novice that he was—demanded his full attention. He had to confess that he liked it when Nicki looked at him and smiled, which he found he could make her do by tickling her under her chin, which he could do without a lot of fuss while Lily's back was turned. He liked doing it then. He didn't feel foolish. And with Lily off across the room, he knew Nicki's smile was for him. That gave him an odd kind of satisfaction.

Odd or not, he needed *some* satisfaction, because with Lily so often close, the breaks were few and far between. He spent the time she was nursing Nicki at the window, looking out at the storm, wishing it would end, wondering when it would, planning the action he'd take when it happened, but no sooner did he return to the center of the room than he felt that same unbidden excitement deep inside. Increasingly that excitement led to a sense of deprivation, which made him testy.

Lily's version of testy was edgy. No matter what other things she thought of, when Quist came near, she was acutely and physically aware of him, and when that happened, she got nervous. She fumbled around his large hands for the diaper tapes, bobbled the can of soup he opened for her to heat, twice lost the stirring spoon in the pot. Though she could blame the clumsiness on her splinted wrist, she knew its true cause.

Quist was exceedingly virile. Everything about him smacked of man, from his height, to his physique, to the gentle bob of his Adam's apple when he drank, the fine hairs on the backs of his hands and the veins on his forearms. His walk, especially, intrigued her. It was tight-hipped and spare of movement, but it got him where he was going just when he wanted to be there. Of course, he wasn't going far within the cabin, but that meant that wherever he did go, she could watch.

It was a trying pastime. Too often, when their eyes met, that special heat flared, and their eyes met often. Sheer boredom led to that. There wasn't much to keep either occupied in a way that was separate from the other. The cabin was too small, their activities too enmeshed.

Lily was taking her turn at the window, looking helplessly out at the storm, when, from out of the blue, she said, "Are you really a cowboy?"

Quist was feeding the stove, whose heat was slightly depleted after having provided them with a lunch of hot soup. Her question made him pause. Twisting on his heels to look back at her, he said, "I thought that was a given."

She came away from the draft. "Are you one?"

He shrugged and turned back to the woodstove, pushing the log where he wanted it. "Depends how you define the term. If you mean, do I live on a ranch with cattle and horses and branding irons and dust, the answer is yes. If you mean, do I swing into the saddle every morning wearing chaps and spurs to do all kinds of fancy tricks with my rope, the answer is no." He closed the grate and stood, brushing his hands against each other. "My ranch is a business. When I'm not in my office, I'm in town contracting for supplies, and when I ride the range, it's usually in a Jeep."

Nothing he said diminished the slightly romantic notion she had of a cowboy and his life. She could see him doing those things. Dark head, bronzed skin, tight hips and long, denim-covered legs—he made a handsome cowboy. "Do you like the work?" she asked and watched him sink into the chair she'd come to think of as his.

"Yes."

"Do you miss it now?"

He stretched out his long legs and nodded.

"Is it nice, Montana?"

He shot her a glance. She was standing by the chair he'd come to think of as hers. "Never been there?"

She shook her head.

"It's real pretty. Green and blue. Lots of wide-open spaces. I like wide-open spaces."

She could imagine he would, given his size. She could picture him standing on his front porch, taking a long, deep breath of the fresh air, then striding easily off toward the corral. He was the commanding type, with the more to command, the better, she guessed.

That raised another issue. "Who's taking care of things while you're gone?"

"I have a foreman."

"Is he good?"

"He's been with me for fourteen years. I trust him." He looked at her again. "Why all the questions?"

She shrugged. "I don't know. I was just wondering. That kind of life is totally foreign to anything I've ever known."

"A city girl born and bred?" he asked with a dry twist to his lips.

"Something wrong with that?" she asked right back. Picking a fight with him was better than panting after him.

"Wrong? That depends on what you want in life. City living's great if you want headaches, stomach aches, traffic jams, lines everywhere you turn and either cockroach-infested apartments or ticky-tacky houses on quarter-acre lots. Me," he took a breath, "I'd die living like that."

She brushed her fingertips on the arm of the chair. "But you did it once."

"Did I tell you that?"

"You said you lived in a triple-decker. I've never heard of a ranch with a triple-decker. You know the pitfalls of city living very well. And then there's the way you talk. You don't talk like a cowboy."

He was amused. "How is a cowboy supposed to talk?"

"With a drawl. With *ain't*s and *dunno*s and *mama*s. And *darlin'*s. You've never called me darlin'." She slipped into the chair and settled back. "If you were a native cowboy, you'd have done that."

He snorted. "You've been watching the wrong programs."

"Cowboys don't use words like that?"

"Some do, some don't. But you're right," he hurried on, because she'd already picked up on too much, "I was born in the city." And once started, it seemed a shame not to tell it all. "We lived in Seattle, my father and me. Then we moved to Denver, then Detroit."

"Why so many moves? Did it have to do with his work?"

"Maybe. He was a restless kind of guy."

"Do you think he was looking for your mother?"

The muscle in his jaw jumped. "If he was, he never told me, and he sure as hell never found her."

Lily was amazed at the anger that the mere mention of his mother stirred in Quist. Not wanting to make things worse, she redirected her questions. "What happened after Detroit?"

"*In* Detroit. He died."

She turned her head against the wood slats to find him staring at the woodstove, not quite angry, but sober. "And?"

"I raised hell for the next four years. Then I won the ranch."

"Won?"

"In a game of five-card stud."

"You're kidding."

Slowly he shook his head.

"You *won* it?"

He nodded.

"Men actually do that—put something as valuable as a ranch up as a stake?"

"Damn right they do," he said, but he remembered how stunned he'd been, himself—no, what had stunned him was the lousy hand the guy had. Poker players were usually more careful when something as vital was at stake. "Not that the ranch was worth a hell of a lot back then, but it was more than I'd ever had." He looked at her. "So I took it."

"That's incredible," she said with a smile of amazement. "And you made it work."

He basked in her smile, letting its warmth seep through him. She was so pretty when she smiled, he thought. No, she was pretty all the time, but when she smiled, she lit up, and that lit him up inside.

Her smile, he realized, was totally innocent, seductive in the broadest sense of the word, and dangerous.

That thought was sobering. In a darker voice, he said, "I made it work, all right. I fought and sweated and bled to get it in shape, and once I'd done that, I fought and sweated and bled some more to get it growing. That place is me."

"Mmm. Big and dark and rough," she teased, but he didn't smile.

"Not dark, but big and rough. It's a man's place."

"Without a woman's touch?"

"Don't need a woman's touch."

"Do the women who see it agree?"

"Women don't see it."

Lily frowned. "Where do you see *them*?"

"Anywhere but the ranch. The ranch is mine. Besides, a ranch is no place for a woman."

Lily stared at him, then made a face. "That's the dumbest thing I've ever heard. Women have lived on ranches since the beginning of time. Who do you think did all the cooking and cleaning and sewing while the cowboys were out getting dirty?"

"Correction," he said, looking back at the fire. "A ranch is no place for the women *I* know. I love it—they'd hate it. I don't need that kind of grief."

Whether it was something in his voice or the grim set of his face that did it, Lily wasn't sure. But she suddenly wondered whether he was afraid of rejection. After all, he'd been rejected early on by his mother.

"Why would they hate it?" she asked more gently.

"It's not fancy. It's not society. It doesn't have four-star restaurants or exciting nightlife. It doesn't have nightlife, period, because the days begin at dawn. It relies heavily on routine. It's quiet and isolated. And peaceful," he tacked on, because that was the way the ranch made him feel.

Lily thought it sounded nice. "What about creature comforts?" she asked, teasing again.

This time, his mouth relaxed into a sheepish half smile. He remembered what he'd told her. "It has those."

"Then maybe it isn't so bad. Maybe you underestimate your women."

His smile went the way of the warmth in his eyes. "No. Never that." He was out of his chair in a minute, stalking to a corner of the kitchen. There, he turned to glare at Lily, who was sitting demurely in her chair. "Don't look at me that way." She didn't blink. "What are you staring at?"

"You. You really do know the wrong women. You're typically male."

"What do you mean by that?"

"Men want women who are fast and free and glitzy. What was it you said—your women are tall, buxom, curvy and blond? It's an ego thing. You think you're hot stuff if you attract hot-shot women." She pictured Jarrod, pictured his new wife, whom she'd known quite well and who was the embodiment of glitz. Then she deliberately blinked them away. "Well, of *course* those women won't fit on a ranch. That's not to say that other women wouldn't do just fine."

"They would not."

"They would, too."

"Ranch life is hard."

"Uh-huh, with your office and your Jeep and your creature comforts."

"Ranch life is *hard*."

"And a woman's too soft?" She heard just about enough. Coming out of her chair, she advanced on him. "You want to believe that. You want to believe it so bad that you keep your eyes closed to the alternative." Her own eyes were angry. "For your information, women can be every bit as hard as men, if not harder. We have to be, if only to survive the mess you guys make of things!"

She whirled away, but he caught her arm and whirled her back. "I've never made a mess of anyone's life—"

"—but your own. You're missing out on a whole lot, Quist, and some day you'll die a lonely old man!" As soon as the words were out, she regretted them, and it had to do only in part with the rigidity of his features. She'd confused the issues, let her own anger jade her judgment. "I'm sorry," she whispered. "I shouldn't have said that. It's not my place to tell you what's right or wrong. I haven't done such a super job with my own life."

Quist wanted to say, "Damned right, you haven't," but the words wouldn't come. He stood there staring at her, wondering how she could be hard and soft at the same time, knowing she was. She was so different. Whether she was being quiet and vulnerable or vocal and insistent, he wanted her.

He could see that she wanted him, too. It was there in her eyes as she stood before him. It was there in the faint tremor that gave her body a gossamer feel, and in the quickening of her breath.

Taking a deep one of his own, with his hand still on her arm, he led her across the room. "We're going out," he muttered.

"Out?" she said shakily. "We were out before, and it's still snowing."

"I need fresh air."

"Then you can go out."

"You need it, too," he said and looked at her in such a way that she didn't say another word. She submitted to being helped on with her boots and her coat. She waited while he put on his own things. Then, holding the back of his coat, she let him lead her out into the storm.

Heads bowed against the wind, they waded through the thigh-high snow to circle the cabin twice before making a stop at the outhouse. Quist, who had that much more strength than Lily and commensurate sexual energy to expel, made two more circles before joining her inside. She'd managed to shrug out of her coat and work her boots off with her feet, but when she turned to him, he caught his breath.

Her hair was still matted by the hood of her coat, and the moss-green sweater she wore didn't exactly go with her pink sweatpants. But her eyes were clear, her cheeks red, her lips moist. She looked good enough to eat.

In the space of a breath he was before her, taking her face in his hands, covering her mouth with his. He kissed her with the hunger he thought he'd just walked off. Then he murmured against her mouth, "This isn't going to work. I want you too much."

Lily moved her hand over his jaw, trying to warm it with a hand that was none too warm, itself. Then, trying to warm her hand, she buried her fingers under the crew neck of his sweater. The skin there was warm and firm, and just that little bit fuzzy.

"Lily," he warned.

"I know," she said quickly and withdrew her hand. "It's okay." She turned from him. "Nicki's due up any minute." Sitting on the mattress beside the drawer, she held her hands in her lap and watched the baby until she awoke.

But Quist was right. It wasn't going to work. No matter how hard she tried to concentrate on the baby, she was aware of him. If it hadn't been for her wrist, she decided, she'd have been able to do everything on her own. But her wrist was broken. So she needed help. And he was more than willing—no, he insisted on giving it.

Afternoon wore into evening. The snow let up a little, which was the only hopeful thing that happened. They continued to struggle with thoughts and looks and accidental touches. Tension ran high between them, and though it was sexually-induced, it took different outlets. Quist snapped at Lily for using up the hot water without telling him; she snapped back at him when he diapered Nicki too loosely; he told her that the bread she'd made to eat with the stew wasn't real bread at all, and she said that it couldn't be since she didn't have yeast, so it was quick bread—and between them they ate every crumb.

By the time Nicki went to sleep at eight o'clock, Lily felt the night had already been endless. She sat by the stove for a bit, then lay down on the mattress and pulled the blanket to her chin. But though she was tired, she couldn't sleep. Her insides were astir with feelings and thoughts that she shouldn't have been feeling or thinking. So she tossed and turned on her mattress.

In time, Quist lowered the lamp and turned in, too, but his rest wasn't any more peaceful than hers. At one point, without considering for a minute that she might be asleep, he growled, "Is it your wrist?"

"Is what my wrist?"

"Whatever it is that's making you squirm."

"No, it's not my wrist."

"Do you have to go to the bathroom?"

"No! I'm restless. That's all."

"You're keeping me up," he alleged.

"You're keeping yourself up," she told him and flopped over again.

Quist was in fact up in the most sexual of senses and had no way to relieve it. He ached to take Lily, but he wouldn't. His body was punishing him for his chivalry.

After long periods of thinking about the ranch, plotting strategies for diversifying his herd and counting the heads of cattle in the pen he drew in his mind, he fell asleep. When he awoke, it was four in the morning, Nicki was whimpering, and he was hard as a rock.

Ignoring the last, though it caused him a moan when he pushed himself up, he went to the drawer, lifted the baby and deposited her into Lily's waiting arms. On impulse, he sat down at the base of the chair and pulled Lily back against him. "Do it here," he said with a huskiness that could have been due to a number of things. "Indulge me."

"Quist . . ."

He fitted her more snugly into the notch of his thighs. "Nothing can happen. You've got Nicki."

On the one hand, he was right. Lily drew up her sweater and put Nicki to her breast, and all was fine. She switched breasts midway through, and all was still fine.

The trouble came when she was done.

7

QUIST CAREFULLY PUT Nicki back in her drawer and watched Lily tuck her in. But when she turned toward her own mattress, he caught her hand and in a single fluid movement had her in his arms.

She barely had time to cry his name when his mouth came down over hers, and what she'd so diligently tried to suppress for so long sprang to life. There was nothing tentative or exploratory about this kiss, nor was it gentle. It was hard and hungry, like Quist's body, and it wasn't about to be denied.

His mouth plundered hers. It slanted and sucked, drawing her deeper into his desire. She was stunned by the force of that desire, stunned even more by the understanding that the desire was her own. She'd never thought of herself as a woman who craved. In times past when she'd been with a man, his needs had directed and dominated the dance. Jarrod had barely cared whether she achieved satisfaction, and, in truth, she hadn't cared much, either. The pleasure was in the giving.

Something was different now. She opened her mouth to Quist, took his tongue and gave her own in return, but the giving was greedy. She'd never felt such hot and intense a need, and though a small voice in her brain warned her to caution, the rest of her didn't listen. She was caught up in sensation and in an irrational but irrevocable feeling that what she was doing was right.

Quist wasn't thinking any more clearly than she was. Holding her head still, he devoured her mouth. He tasted her, drank her, breathed her until even that wasn't enough. Sliding his arms around her body, he crushed her to him with a force that made Lily cry out.

Immediately he loosened his hold. "Are you okay?"

"I think so," she said with a breathless little laugh. When he backed into the chair he'd just left and brought her down on his lap, she whispered a hurried, "Maybe we shouldn't, Quist." Her arms, even the one with the splinted wrist, were draped over his shoulders, and though she was having trouble catching her breath, her eyes held his.

"We have to," he answered. Voice, gaze, touch—all smoldered with barely banked heat. "We have to. I can't explain the need," it was as much emotional as physical, as much a need to stake a claim as to slake a desire, "but it's too strong." He took her head in his hands. "I need you, Lily. I'm making you mine."

Like the fierceness of his kiss, the boldness of his words excited her. He didn't ask. He didn't beg. He told her what was going to happen and why, and since Lily was feeling everything he was, she couldn't argue with his conclusion. Instead, her body began to tremble in anticipation.

He kissed her again until she was gasping for breath. Then he brought the hem of her sweater up and took it over her head and off, leaving her naked above the waist. He held her back to look at her, first her eyes, then for a long time her breasts.

Her breath came more shallowly. She was acutely aware of her nakedness, of the rapid rise and fall of her breasts, of their heaviness, of the paleness ribboned by veins that had come with motherhood, and she might have tried to cover herself if it hadn't been for the look in his eyes. That look was incredible. It made her feel warm and beautiful. And sexy. No man had ever made her feel sexy like that. Not a word, just that look, and she soared.

But the soaring had just begun. When he put his hands on her breasts, she sucked in a breath. She let it out in a soft sigh of pleasure when he began to knead her flesh, and when he lowered his head and took a distended nipple into his mouth, she cried out.

He paused, fearful again that he'd hurt her, but she pushed her fingers in his hair and urged him back to her breast. He lingered there just long enough to drive her wild before relinquishing the wet nub to his fingers and moving on to the next. Small sounds of pleasure came from deep in her throat. She urged him closer, then closer still as the crux of the heat moved downward. Pressing her legs together didn't help. Neither did shifting her hips.

Clutching fistfuls of his hair, she whispered his name and tugged. He lifted his head and looked at her, still with the desire and appreciation that made her feel so wanted. The wanting made her desperate.

"I'm on fire," she cried brokenly. "Help me."

He didn't need further urging. His hands went to her sweatpants and pushed them down. He shifted her until the heavy material was free of her hips, then her legs, leaving her in the V-shaped scrap of silk and lace that he found so sexy. With the flat of his hand he touched her stomach, her hips, the small of her back, her bottom, and by the time he returned to her front, he'd breached the barrier of her panties to find the dampness that gave proof to her arousal.

Lily hadn't been so indifferent to satisfaction in the past that she'd never had an orgasm. She knew the feeling, knew when it was imminent, and at that moment she was on the edge. If Quist touched her more deeply, if he slid a finger inside she'd come, and she didn't want to. Not without feeling the iron of him, not without knowing that they were fully coupled.

"Your sweater," she cried against his mouth as she grabbed a handful of it and pulled. More than ever before, she wished for two good hands. Fortunately, Quist had them.

Setting her on her feet, he rose and tore off his sweater. She barely had time to reacquaint herself with the marvel of his chest when he had his zipper down, then his jeans. When he came back to her, he was buck naked and magnificent. Kneeling, he slid her panties down, leaned forward and put his mouth to the hair that was still too short to curl.

Her knees buckled. She slid down until her breasts grazed his chest, and he lowered her to the mattress. His breathing was rough; his arms shook with the force of his desire as he held himself above her, poised between her widely parted thighs.

"Hurry," she whispered and lifted toward him. She was frantic to have him where it seemed he belonged. That sense of rightness had survived the fire of foreplay and was as strong, if not stronger than ever.

But he held back. He looked into her eyes, looked deeper, into her soul and felt touched to the core of his being. She was his. She was bare before him, inside and out. He felt responsible for her, and while he'd always before shunned responsibility where women were concerned, this time he welcomed it. It made him feel possessive, protective and strong. It was also humbling, so much so that instead of thrusting hard into her as his body was telling him to do, he moved forward more gently.

Lily would never know how he'd known to do that, but it was another thing to marvel at. She was tight. She hadn't realized how much so. Involuntarily her body tensed at his initial incursion and she gasped.

"I'm hurting you," he whispered against her temple.

"No. It's . . . from the baby . . . I'm very . . ."

Sealing her mouth with his lips, he began to caress her, first her breasts, then her belly, then the small bud that had hardened between her legs. Little by little, he pressed inside as he built her arousal to an ever higher pitch. He moved his hips in slow, gentle circles, stretching her, allowing her to get used to his size. Only when he was fully buried inside her, when he felt her tightness hugging him to the hilt, did he allow himself a moment's selfishness. Closing his eyes, he arched his long torso, threw his head back and shuddered with pleasure, then, unable to help himself, gave a low cry of triumph.

The triumph was Lily's, too. She'd never felt so much a part of a man, and it wasn't just that Quist was more man than she'd ever met. There was something else. They shared a special feeling. She couldn't comprehend the extent of it just then, because all that was happening inside was near to overwhelming, but she was more satisfied by what they were doing than she'd ever been by any orgasm.

Sensing and sharing that satisfaction, Quist held himself still. After a time, he breathed in a long, shaky breath, opened his eyes and looked down at her. What he saw made his heart pound harder against his ribs.

Lily's gray eyes were warm and velvet and there was a soft smile on her lips. Her cheeks were pink, her skin dewy. Her breasts rose and fell with the short breaths she took, while her knees hugged his sides. She looked as though she'd be perfectly content to stay right where she was for an eternity, and he wasn't sure he'd have minded. She was without a doubt the most beautiful, the most serene, the most honest woman he'd ever made love to.

He gave a small smile. "Ahh, Lily." When her brows rose in question, he whispered, "I could almost be tempted to look at you like this all day." Bowing his head, he opened his mouth on her neck and gave her the hickey he'd promised.

"You rat," she whispered back, but her smile grew wider. "Haven't you got better things to do with your mouth?" Coming up off the mattress, she used her own on his nipple. When he let out a guttural cry, she wound her arms around his neck and gave him the kind of kiss that made him think of all those better things he could do.

He did a good many of them in the next few minutes, and if there were some that he missed, neither of them noticed. Laying her down, he made love to her fully—withdrawing and gently reentering, withdrawing and coming back harder, withdrawing and thrusting home with the force of his ardor.

Lily egged him on. Once past her initial tenderness, she was a creature she'd never known. She writhed in response to the fire he lit and demanded he tend it. It never occurred to her to lie still, as a vessel for his pleasure; that simply wasn't part of their relationship. With Quist, she was a free agent, a woman letting herself blossom without set rules or preconceptions. He was a rough-edged man prone to wild passion, and wild passion was what he inspired. She gave and she took with rapturous fury.

Their bodies grew sweaty as they worked toward a near-violent crest. At its height, she felt a moment's fear, the sensation was so intense. His name was a frantic cry on her lips, but he was fast to soothe her.

"That's it, Lily," he panted, pumping more quickly. "Let it come. Let go for me. That's it."

Catching in a breath, she arched up off the mattress, closed her eyes and went very still for an instant before erupting into a series of shuddering spasms. She was still in their grip when Quist thrust deeper than ever. With a low, agonized sound, he gained his release—but not before he'd found the wherewithal to pull out of her.

Lily missed him instantly. Though their damp bodies remained entwined, she felt a sudden and stark emptiness inside. It brought tears to her eyes. "Quist?" she whispered, still breathless from the power of what she'd experienced.

It was a minute before the harshness of his breathing eased, another before he raised his head from her shoulder. One look at the tears in her eyes and he said, "Oh, no, don't do that." He brushed the moisture from her lids with his mouth. "Don't cry. Not now."

"Why did you do that? It was so perfect until that."

He'd been afraid she regretted having made love and was deeply relieved it wasn't so. Shifting to cradle her gently against him, he lifted her splinted wrist to his chest. Then he ran his thumb under her eyes to catch the tears that remained. "You've just had a baby," he said and felt protective. "You don't want another so soon."

Lily was surprised; thought of birth control hadn't entered her mind. In self-defense, she said, "I wouldn't have gotten pregnant. It was just one time."

His smile was indulgent, the rolling of his eyes more eloquent than that. So she tried again.

"A woman can't get pregnant while she's nursing."

"Is that a fact? Has it never happened? Not once?"

"Well, maybe once or twice," she conceded, "but those are the exceptions."

He studied her face, stroked her damp cheek. "Look at you," he said, feeling concern this time. "You have a new baby and no home. Can you even begin to imagine what it would be like to be pregnant on top of that?"

It would be terrifying, she knew, still she felt the same emptiness she'd felt when he'd first withdrawn. "I liked being pregnant," she said almost as an afterthought and lowered her face to his chest. He had a nice chest. It was firm and well shaped and had just enough hair to lightly cushion her cheek. Besides, his chest held his heart, and its steady beat was a comfort by her ear.

Looking over the crown of her head to the ivory skin that extended below it, Quist felt a swell of affection. She was so incredibly sweet, sweet to taste, to smell, to hold. And she said sweet things. No other woman had ever complained when he'd put on a rubber. He hadn't had a rubber here, but he'd deliberately waited until she'd climaxed to reach his own peak and withdraw. Still, she was sorry he'd left. That made him feel special.

In fact, he was feeling special in lots of ways. And relaxed. And content. Which was really odd, given the cabin and the storm and the fact that he still had to find his way out of it. Still, at that particular moment, he felt special.

"Quist?"

When she used that tentative tone, he knew something was up. "Mmm?"

"Do you really think I'm sexy?" she asked, keeping her eyes on the lean plane of his middle.

"How can you ask that, after what we just did?"

"For all I know, you go wild with every woman you bed."

He rolled on top of her, partly to feel her again that way and partly to set her straight. "I like sex, and I like it hard and fast. But I've never done what we just did."

All eyes, she looked up at him. "What do you mean?"

He couldn't answer at first, because he wasn't sure *what* he'd meant. Then again, he was. What he'd done with Lily had been more than sex. It had been lovemaking. He couldn't tell her that, though, because she might get the wrong idea. She might think he loved her, and it wasn't that at all. He liked her, liked her in some ways that weren't at all physical, so that when he'd taken her physically, he'd felt more than usual. But like wasn't love. And she was waiting for an answer.

Wrapping himself in the velvet of her gaze, he said in a voice vibrant with attraction, "I've never entered a woman slowly, the way I entered you. I've never really cared if she was uncomfortable at first." He stopped for an instant. "I've never taken a virgin before."

"I'm no virgin," she whispered, cheeks going pink.

"But I imagine it was like that. You were new. You haven't been touched since the baby." He thought about that and slid halfway to her side so that she wouldn't bear the brunt of his weight. Then he asked in a quiet voice, "You were cut there, weren't you?"

She nodded. They'd just made love, which was as intimate as two people could get, still his question seemed even more so. His interest made her warm all over.

"Did it hurt?"

"There was local anesthesia. I didn't feel it."

"Afterward?"

"I felt it then, but it didn't bother me. It was part of having Nicki. I'd do it again in a minute."

"In a minute?"

She smiled. "Well, maybe not so fast, but I wouldn't hesitate to have more children."

"You really enjoyed being pregnant?"

She nodded, and Quist believed her. It was in keeping with everything else she'd said. Besides, she didn't lie. He'd already learned that, though at times like this he wished it weren't so. She was looking up at him with such guileless warmth that he felt his blood stir. Slowly, inevitably, his gaze fell from her face. He moved to see her body better, and when the visual wasn't enough, he touched her.

His hands were large, his fingers callused but gentle. The heady combination sparked a renewed tingling deep in Lily's belly. Grabbing his hand, she dragged it to her throat and held it there.

"What's wrong?" he asked.

She took in a shaky breath. "You touch me and I start to burn. I don't know what it is about you, Quist. I was never like this before."

He seized her mouth to still her words, which were as much a turn-on as anything else. But a taste of her mouth led to a taste of her neck, then one breast, then her stomach. She'd released his hand by then and was touching him wherever she could, and by the time he straightened beside her, he was feeling hot and bothered. Taking her hand, he lowered it on his body. "Touch me," he whispered hoarsely. "I've dreamed of having your hands on me here—" He groaned the last as he curled her fingers around his arousal. Oh, yes, he'd dreamed of that; it was why he'd been so hard when Nicki's cries had woken him. But the dream paled in comparison to reality. He hadn't dared to dream that Lily's fingers would take him higher, and with such untutored skill.

The skill was a product of instinct, in turn a product of curiosity and desire. Lily was intrigued by the length and strength of him. She explored his thickness, the velvety tip and the heaviness beneath, and felt pride when he grew even harder.

His low moan brought her gaze to his face. In the dim light filtering from the woodstove, she saw that it was covered by a sheen of sweat. His eyes were closed, his mouth drawn into a thin line as he struggled to retain a measure of control.

She wanted him to lose it. To that end, she grew even bolder with her hand and her mouth. Tasting his body, brushing her nose through the hair on his chest, dragging her lips along the line that tapered to his navel while she continued to caress his hardness—he was soon breathing roughly, and she wasn't doing much better. Everything about him turned her on. She felt a flame inside that was every bit as hot as it had been not so many minutes before.

Wanting to see how far she'd go, Quist drew her on top of him. Knowing she couldn't put weight on her left wrist, he supported her under each arm. Her legs straddled his hips, and for a prolonged minute of torture, she held herself just inches above him while, taking short, shimmering breaths, she looked down into his eyes. Then, closing her own, she let her hips settle, taking him fully in one smooth glide.

Quist felt possessed. It was a turnaround, but he wasn't displeased. He filled Lily, yet he was the one who felt filled, and the filling was with an almost unbelievable pleasure. It smacked of oneness, which was something he didn't know much about. But like Lily, he acted on instinct, and that instinct was to help her, to make her movements his own, make her rapture high.

At first, he did nothing more than lightly run his hands over her body. When she began to undulate with him inside, he drew her forward so that he could love her breasts with his mouth, and when she dropped her weight to her elbows, he grasped her hips. Guidance or caress—the line blurred, and it didn't matter, because neither of them was analyzing what happened. Instinct and sensation dominated the thrusting sweep of their bodies, and if instinct and sensation were in turn dominated by a deeper underlying emotion, neither of them was analyzing that, either.

They burned, then exploded. In the end, Quist rolled over Lily and afforded her the same protection he'd given the first time. Though she knew what he was doing this time, she still felt the loss, but the heat of her climax carried her through until he held her tightly to his side again.

There were no words when it was over, nothing to describe what had happened. Their bodies continued to communicate for a time, lying limply, then more peacefully entwined. When Quist drew up the blanket, they fell asleep. Neither one of them moved again until Nicki's small cries broke through the morning silence.

Lily stirred first, trying to burrow more snugly against the warmth of Quist's large body. When she realized what the sound was that had awoken her, she started to turn, but he held her still.

"I'll get her." His voice was groggy, and, contrary to his words, he drew her in closer and buried his face in her hair.

Nicki cried again.

"I'd better go," Lily whispered.

But with a kiss to the top of her head, he disengaged himself from her body. "Stay here. I'll bring her over."

Settling her head on the pillow, Lily watched him climb out from under the blanket. His body was beautiful, not only in the throes of passion but now in the morning's light. What she'd only felt earlier she could finally see, most notably the masculine make of his legs and the way his sex lay amid a dark nest of hair. He was impressive in any state of arousal, a pleasure to look at.

But he was reaching for his pants, threatening to deny her that pleasure.

"What are you doing?" she asked, vying with Nicki to make herself heard.

He balanced precariously on one foot as he tried to get the other into his jeans. "I can't very well go to her like this." He glanced down at himself.

Lily was torn between admiration of his body and amusement. "Why not?"

"She's a girl. She could be traumatized."

"She's just a baby. She won't see a thing."

"She sees," he said earnestly, as though he had great insight into the matter. "She understands more than you think."

Pressing her lips together to stifle a grin, Lily gave a slow but confident shake of her head.

He paused. "No?"

She repeated the slow headshake.

"But I'm a strange man. She doesn't know me. I'm not even her father."

"She knows you better than she does her father," Lily said, "but that's neither here nor there. The fact is that she won't know whether you're naked or not, and I don't want you dressed."

That brought a softer look to Quist's face. Nicki kept on crying, but he stayed still where he was with his jeans on one leg and no more. "You don't?"

She shook her head.

"Are you sure?"

She nodded.

Nicki's cries grew more strident. Shucking the jeans, Quist strode to where she lay and picked her up. She quieted right away, which made him grin. "Like that, do ya?" he asked the child in a voice that was light, a little playful, very masculine. "Are you a sexy little thing like your mama?" He placed her carefully in Lily's arms.

"I'm not sexy," Lily chided in a half whisper. Turning onto her side, she put Nicki to her breast.

After fueling the stove, Quist pulled the blanket up to cover Lily's back and stretched out, propping himself on an elbow, to watch her nurse. "What do you mean, you're not sexy?"

"I'm not."

"Sure could've fooled me. Sure could've fooled my body."

Lily felt a heat rise in her cheeks, but she kept her eyes on Nicki. Quist watched them both. He thought of the first time he'd seen her nursing and remembered how uncomfortable he'd felt. He was jealous then. He saw a closeness that he'd never had, and irrationally, he was jealous. That jealousy had eased, mostly because he'd become involved with Lily. Now when she nursed Nicki, it was a specific, rather than a generic activity. But there were still times when he felt pangs of something else, when he looked at the two of them and the warmth they shared and ached to be part of it.

This was one of those times. To get his mind off the aching, he asked, "What does that feel like?"

"It's peaceful," Lily said, smiling into Nicki's eyes. "And very satisfying."

"I mean physically. When she sucks. Is it like when I do it?"

The color in her cheeks deepened. After a minute, she raised her eyes to his. Her voice was feminine without being seductive. "It's the same, but it's different."

"Explain that." When she sent him a pleading look, he said in a voice that was masculine without being seductive, "I want to know."

"But it's hard to explain, and it's embarrassing. Here I am, at the same time nursing my baby and thinking about a man doing . . . putting . . ."

"Sucking." His mouth twitched. "Spit it out, Lily. No need to play prim. After all, you're the woman who insisted I stay naked."

"You keep me warm when you're naked." She looked at his chest. "Besides, I liked what we were doing."

"We were sleeping."

"Before that," she said and took a breath. He was right. There was no reason to be prim, after what they'd done with and to each other. Meeting his eyes again, she said, "The difference between what you do and what Nicki does is in intent and outcome. When Nicki nurses, the sucking sensation brings out maternal things like love and pride and protectiveness. The satisfaction is in the doing. When you, uh, do the same thing, it makes me want more."

He grinned. "Does it now?"

She nodded, and for several minutes, they simply looked at each other, neither one of them saying a word. Finally, with a bit of the devil in it, his grin broadened. "There. You did a real good job with that explanation."

Lily was entranced by his grin. It made him look younger, less stern, almost happy, and the bit of the devil in it was highly endearing. Without thinking, she raised her splinted wrist and touched the tips of her fingers to his chin. He took her hand and gently held it to his neck.

"How does it feel?" he asked.

"Rough. A little stubbly. Very manly."

"Not my chin. Your wrist."

"Oh. Okay."

He sighed. "What does 'okay' mean?"

"Better than yesterday."

"Still ache?"

"A little. It's more an annoyance than anything."

He lightly rubbed her arm just above the splint. "First priority when we hit civilization is a hospital. A cast will be neater and easier to manage than this."

When we hit civilization. The words echoed in Lily's mind, but they didn't have the element of relief they'd had twenty-four hours before. She was feeling safe just where she was, she realized. Safe and happy. Holding Nicki, looking at Quist, it suddenly occurred to her that she wouldn't mind it a bit if they were snowbound for months.

But that made her stop and listen, and what she heard was silence. Eyes widening, she glanced toward the window, then looked back at Quist. "It's over?"

"Sounds it," he said calmly. Rather than getting up to check, he waited to see what she was going to say next.

She didn't say anything at first. She looked down at Nicki, lowered her head and rubbed her cheek against the baby's hair in an attempt to recapture the sense of solidarity she shared with Nicki. They were a twosome, mother and daughter. They'd gone through nine months and five weeks together. They'd left Hartford to make a new life for themselves, and that was just what they'd do.

Now, though, there was Quist. She wasn't sure where he fit into the life they were making, but it had to be somewhere. He was too special; what she'd done with him was too intimate. Even if their relationship proved to be nothing more than an aberration, a product of being caught together in an isolated cabin in the midst of a blizzard, she'd remember him. She wasn't sure she was ready to say goodbye.

When she raised her eyes to his, they were filled with tears. "We were just starting to have fun," she whispered.

Quist didn't know whether to laugh or cry. He'd been thinking the same thing, but hadn't wanted to say it. "Don't you dare go weepy on me now."

"If the snow's stopped, you'll be leaving."

"I don't know for sure that it's stopped."

"Aren't you going to look?"

"Me? And freeze my butt off? I'm not dressed." He took a lazy breath. "Maybe later."

"But you said you'd have to set off first thing in the morning," she argued. Even as she did it, though, something in his expression registered. He was looking a little too content, almost to the point of smugness. Slowly the meaning of the look set in. He was giving them an extra day. "Thank you," she whispered, and this time the tears that welled were ones of happiness.

Quist wanted to scold her, but couldn't. Her tears, he was learning, were as expressive of what she was feeling as a laugh or a sigh or a moan. They came and went quickly, and were eminently honest. He couldn't fault her for that, particularly since in this case she was crying because she was pleased to be spending another day with him.

He wondered what was going to happen when the time came for them to part. It wouldn't be the lightest of moments, he knew, and determined to push it out of his mind.

Actually that was easily done. Once Nicki was fed, they did dress to make a trip to the outhouse. The snow had stopped, and the forest was beautiful, which added to the idyllic feeling they brought back into the cabin with them. While Lily played with Nicki, Quist put together a breakfast that, while it wasn't quite as imaginative as Lily's had been, filled their stomachs. When they were done, he helped her bathe the baby, and when they were done with that and Nicki had been rocked and sung to and put in for a nap, they bathed themselves. All three baths were a joint effort. The last two led to something far hotter than the water.

"I've never been like this in my life," Lily murmured when, once again, they lay sweaty and spent in each other's arms. "You've corrupted me."

Quist gave a weak laugh, which was all he could muster after the physical exertion he'd just made. "I think you got that backward. You're the corrupter. I'm just an innocent cowboy."

"For an innocent cowboy, you sure know how to do some naughty things."

He opened an eye and looked down at her. "And you loved them. Admit it. You loved them."

"I admit it," she said simply. Pressing a kiss on his chest, she put her head down. "This is all so unreal," she breathed.

"Mmm."

"Hard to believe how we met."

"Hard to believe what we've done since we met."

She laughed softly, almost to herself, but the laugh quickly died. She was thinking that it would be a story for the books, one to tell the grandchildren, only she didn't know whose grandchildren she'd tell. She and Quist wouldn't have any together.

"Quist?"

"Mmm?"

"When do you think you'll leave?"

He was quiet for a time. Finally he said, "Tomorrow. You ought to have your wrist casted right, Nicki's running out of diapers and I'm getting sick of hash."

He was right on all counts, she knew. She also knew that she'd give just about anything to stay another day, then another day after that. But it couldn't be. He had to leave. Thought of that brought new worries.

"The snow's deeper now than when we hiked in here. The going will be tough."

"I've got long legs."

"But you may get lost."

"I'll follow the break in the trees, same way I did to get us here, and I won't have the wind and the snow."

"What about animals? They'll be out foraging for food. I think I read somewhere that there are bears in northern Maine."

"They're in hibernation." Taking her chin, he tipped her face to his. "I'll be okay, Lily."

"I'll worry."

"But I'll be okay. And you will be, too."

Lily wasn't so sure. The thought of Quist leaving, of his being gone for a long time gave her a desolate feeling. She was going to have to learn to live with it, she supposed, but that didn't mean it wasn't real.

"Kiss me," she whispered, wanting a little forgetfulness.

He gave her that and more, then repeated the good deed while Nicki was napping that afternoon. He might have been sick of hash, but his appetite for Lily was endless, so much so that he was almost willing to consider staying put for another day when the decision was taken out of his hands. The sound of an engine broke through the silence of the forest, waking him from a doze. Slipping out of Lily's arms, he went to the window in time to see the arrival of a pair of snowmobiles.

In an instant he was back shaking Lily's shoulder. "Up you go, sweetheart. We've got company." He was into his pants in a flash, then helped Lily into hers. She had just managed to pull on a sweater when the door burst open.

Their guests, it seemed, weren't guests at all, but the son of the owner of the cabin and his girlfriend. It was a toss-up as to who was the most uncomfortable—Lily and Quist for having been caught in the love nest they had created, or the two younger lovers who had come to create their own.

Civilization, it seemed, was an hour away by snowmobile. With a little arm twisting, Quist managed to convince his male counterpart to return with him for help. Leaving the young girl with Lily, and feeling better that she wasn't alone, he set off.

Shortly before dark he returned with a snowplow and its driver, the boy and his snowmobiles, plus two gallons of gas.

8

THE NEXT FEW HOURS passed in something of a blur for Lily. With Quist's help—and that of the young girl, who was anxious to see them gone and be alone with her boy-friend—she neatened the cabin and repacked the things they'd carried through the snow. Strapping Nicki to her chest, she climbed into the cab of the truck to sit between the driver and Quist.

The distance to the car was no more than four miles. What had taken Lily and Quist more than three hours to trek through on foot in the storm took the snowplow thirty minutes. Between the two men, the Audi was shoveled off, towed onto the newly plowed path, gassed up and warmed in another thirty minutes. By the time darkness was complete, Lily and Quist were following the truck back to town.

Quist drove. With his Stetson on his head and the collar of his sheepskin jacket up, he looked so much like the distant cowboy she'd picked up in the storm that Lily felt lonely again. Occasionally he glanced at her, but the night masked his expression. Only once, when he reached out to touch her, did she feel a breath of the warmth they'd shared.

He stopped in town to settle up with the driver of the snowplow and make arrangements to have his abandoned rental car retrieved and returned to an agency outlet. Then, as promised, he set off for the nearest hospital. It turned out to be an hour north of where they'd emerged from the woods. Nicki, who had awoken hungry halfway through the drive, was already fed by the time they arrived, and again, Quist took charge. Holding the baby like a pro, he ushered Lily inside, had an X ray taken and an orthopedist examining her arm before she'd had time to do more than fill out a cursory form, and while Nicki slept in his arms, he watched the doctor put a lightweight, waterproof cast on Lily's wrist.

Back in the Audi, parked under the bright lights of the emergency entrance, Quist turned to her. His voice was deep, quiet. "Quebec is four hours north of here. It's ten now. We could be there by two. Or we can find a place to spend the night and make the drive in the morning." He watched her closely, trying to look through the frail mask of her defenses. Cautiously he said, "I say we find a place. I want a hot shower and a big bed. How about it?"

He'd read her well, she mused with a smile and a nod. She was feeling tired, though she didn't know why she should, since she and Quist had dozed on and off for a good part of the day. Perhaps more than tired, she was drained. Leaving the security of the cabin had thrown her once more into the limbo of her life. Finding a room somewhere, with four walls and Quist, sounded just right.

What they found, actually, was a ski lodge that had plenty of midweek vacancies. They took one room; there was never any question of taking a second. Quist registered in his name, and if the clerk chose to assume that they were a family, that was fine. All they asked of him was the room key and a portable crib, both of which he produced without pause.

The room wasn't fancy, but it was warm, carpeted and blessed with a king-size bed. Nicki was quickly changed and put into the portable crib, and while Lily rubbed her back to help her fall asleep, Quist took the shower he'd been dying to have. When he'd finished, he came back for her.

Reluctant to wet her cast until it had fully hardened, Lily opted for a bath, and nothing, she swore, nothing had ever felt so good—at least, that was what she told Quist, who was helping her at every turn. The fact that he made her feel better than the bath was something she kept to herself. She wasn't sure whether he'd take it as calculated flattery, and she didn't want that.

What she wanted was to go to Montana with him. She wasn't sure when she'd gotten the idea, but it had come to her and stuck like glue. But she knew what he thought of women, in general, and women on a ranch, in particular. Granted, he had to know by now that she wasn't a piece of fluff, still she had to be careful. She couldn't do anything to suggest she was trying to manipulate him. If she was to go to Montana, the idea had to come from him.

So she simply smiled her pleasure as she floated in the hot bath water. He helped her soap up, even washed her hair, and by the time he'd finished drying her off, the towel he'd wrapped around his hips was too small.

They made love on the clean sheets of the king-size bed, and even apart from the cleanliness of the bed and their bodies, the experience was new and different, special in ways that Lily couldn't begin to name. Hunger, greed, joy, desperation—so many things entered into their mating that it was hard to sort one from the other. The past was a dream, the future an enigma, yet they were affected by both. And in the aftermath, when Lily lay with her head and an arm on his chest and a slender leg between his longer, more ropey ones, she knew that she loved him.

Morning came all too soon. Though they lingered in the waking, taking time with Nicki and each other, and then lingered over breakfast in a nearby coffee shop, inevitably they had to drive on.

It was midafternoon when they reached Quebec. Again Quist took a room, this time at the Hilton, which, he told Lily, had a shopping arcade so that she'd have something to do while he was out taking care of business. Lily wanted to tell him that she didn't like shopping, and that she'd be glad to go with him to confront the half sister he'd never seen, and that if anything she ought to be looking for an apartment for Nicki and herself.

She didn't tell him any of those things, not because they weren't true, but because he was gone before she'd had a chance.

So she stayed in the room to feed and change Nicki, and by the time she was done, it was too late to start apartment hunting. Besides, she wanted to be there when Quist returned, if only she knew when that would be. He had an address, she knew, but whether he'd find his half sister there, or whether he'd have to go elsewhere, and if he did find her how long they'd spend talking, Lily didn't know.

The complicating factor, of course, was that Lily didn't know quite where she stood with Quist, and that was the one thing that made her most uneasy as the minutes piled up. Playing with Nicki was a distraction and a comfort, but when Nicki began to doze off, the distraction was gone. So she bathed. With the comfort and compactness of the cast on her wrist, she had greater use of her fingers than she'd had before. She brushed her hair until it shone, put on the smallest bit of makeup, dressed in a sweater and skirt. Frustrated with the waiting, she put a sleeping Nicki into the carrier, slid the straps over her shoulders, anchoring the baby to her front, and went down to sit in the lobby and wait for Quist there.

He returned ninety minutes after he'd left. Lily saw him instantly as he strode from the revolving door. Even without the Stetson, which he held in his hand, he stood head and shoulders above the rest, but he didn't look pleased.

Hurrying to join him, she weathered a tense glance as they stepped into the elevator. He didn't say a word, simply punched their floor then stood with his jaw set and his eyes on the digital readout. With other people in the car she knew he wouldn't talk, but once they reached the privacy of their own room, she waited apprehensively.

He stalked to the window, pulled back the sheer and stared at the night lights of the city.

"Quist?" she prodded.

Slowly he turned and in an equally slow but very angry voice said, "She wasn't there. At the first place they sent me to a second, and at the second they sent me to a third. At the third place they told me she'd left town." His nostrils flared with the carefully controlled breath he took. "She left town. I came all this goddamned way, lost three days in a damned blizzard, not to mention the two days I spent checking out New York and Boston, and she left town."

Lily gave a small moan of disappointment. "When?"

"Day before yesterday."

"In the storm?"

"They said it wasn't so bad here. She probably figured she'd use it to her benefit by getting a jump on anyone who might be on her tail." He thrust a hand through his hair, then hooked both hands on his hips and scowled. "If I'd have gotten here when I was supposed to, I'd have caught her, and if I'd have done that, I'd be back home right now."

"And if I hadn't taken the wrong turns," Lily put in, because she knew he was thinking it, "you'd have gotten here when you were supposed to." She paused. "I'm sorry, Quist. I messed you up."

"Women always mess me up," he grumbled without acknowledging her apology. "I'm the man, but they're the ones doing the screwing. I haven't met a woman yet who was good for her word. Jennifer calls me and asks if I'll come— I come and she's gone. She's just like her mother. Runs away and keeps running. I don't know why I thought it would be any different."

Lily didn't like being lumped with his women, particularly since she'd been honest from the first. But the argument was better saved for later. When it came to anything to do with his mother, and Jennifer had to do with his mother, he was raw. "Did they say where she'd gone?"

"Chicago."

"Chicago!"

"That's what I said."

"What's she going to do in Chicago?"

"Same thing she was going to do here, I guess—hide out until things quiet down."

"But if you were able to find out where she's headed, so will whoever it is who's following her."

He shook his head. "She had protective friends. I had to show an ID to get the information. At least she had enough brains to give them my name and say I'd be coming. But what in the hell does she expect me to do, follow her all over the goddamned northern hemisphere?" Swearing again, he turned back to the window.

Lily took in the rigid set of his shoulders and his tight stance, and although the circumstances were completely different, she couldn't help but remember when they'd first met. He'd been angry then, too—at himself for falling asleep at the wheel, at her for being a woman picking him up in a sporty red car, at the world for stranding him on a mountain road, at whatever it was that had made it snow.

She'd been able to shrug off his anger then, because she hadn't known him at all. She knew him now, though, and it bothered her to see him upset. Slipping her arms out of the carrier, and laying Nicki in the center of the bed, she went to him.

"What will you do?" she asked in a softer voice. When he didn't answer, she put a tentative hand on his back, and when he didn't move away, she slid it up and began to lightly massage his shoulder. "She's young. Probably frightened and confused."

"She should have stayed put," he growled, "I told her I'd come."

"But she doesn't know you. Maybe she's as wary of men as you are of women."

"Then she shouldn't have called me in the first place."

"But you're her half brother. You may be the only living relative she has."

"Does that give her the right to use me?"

"It gives her the right to ask for your help. You could have refused her at the start."

"I should have."

"Why didn't you?"

"Because she's my half sister," he snapped. "She may be the only living relative *I* have."

Which said a lot, Lily mused. It said that though Quist didn't have family, he wanted it, and that made her love him all the more. Unable to help herself, she slid an arm around his waist and fitted herself to his side. "You're a softy, do you know that?"

"I've never been a softy," he muttered.

"Maybe not on the outside, but inside—" she flattened a hand on his chest "—you've got heart."

"I won't be taken advantage of."

"Who's trying to?"

He hesitated for a minute before shooting her a look. "You. I know what you're thinking. You're thinking that if I've come this far, I owe it to myself to go to Chicago. It's on the way home, if I was driving. But I'm not, and you know it."

"I wasn't thinking that at all, but since you mention it, it's not such a bad idea."

"She could be gone when I get there. This has been a wild-goose chase so far. Who's to say Chicago isn't just the next bogus stop?"

"Can you call her first? I assume you have an address. Do you have a phone number?"

"No, and I can't get one. She's staying with a friend. I have the address but no name, and the lady I spoke with didn't know it."

"Chicago is on the way."

"Not as the crow flies."

"But as American or Delta or TWA flies. You could easily stop there on the way home."

He grimaced. "Damn it, I shouldn't have to do that."

"What's your alternative? After you've gone through all this, can you really go home and forget about her? Won't you always wonder what happened? Won't you wonder whether she got into trouble? Won't you feel guilty that maybe you weren't there when she needed you?"

"I *was* there, but she *moved*," he argued, feeling more frustrated than anything else.

Quietly, Lily said, "You'll always wonder, Quist."

He stared at her hard. "You're laying a guilt trip on me."

"No. I'm trying to put into words what you won't. You make yourself out to be a callous kind of guy, but you're not that at all. And I think that if you don't follow this thing through, you'll always wonder if you should've."

He continued to stare at her, but the hardness was easing. "You're being manipulative."

"Me? Manipulative?" She'd tried so hard not to be. "How am I being manipulative?"

"Your words. Your tone. They're so damned reasonable. And the way you've got yourself plastered to my side—how can I think straight when you do that?"

She started to move away, but he tugged her right back, and then it was his long arm that sandwiched her in. "If you're such a tough guy," she said, tipping up a defensive chin, "you should be able to withstand anything I do. And while we're on the subject," she grabbed at a breath, "I want to make a couple of things clear. I am not a manipulative woman, nor have I ever tried to take advantage of you—" her voice dropped "—well, maybe I did when we first met, because I thought you could help me if I got stuck in the snow, but after that plan fell through, I wasn't thinking at all in terms of what I could get out of you." She paused to recoup, and her voice rose again. "And the fact that I'm telling you this should make my next point. I've never lied to you. I've never gone back on my word. So don't group me with women you've known in the past. It's not my fault you're a lousy picker of women."

Finished, she closed her mouth, but in the next blink it was open again. "If it hadn't been for the storm, we'd never have met. If you'd seen me on the street, you wouldn't have looked twice. You've said it yourself, I'm not your type. Well, I say 'hallelujah' because it doesn't sound to me like your type is so hot."

Held captive by the vibrancy of her features, Quist felt a swelling in the area of his heart. Lily was unreal, that was all there was to it. She was a vision he'd conjured up to fill the void in his life—which was truly remarkable, since before this trip he hadn't given great thought to that void. She was sweet and agreeable, industrious, domesticated, feisty when she felt he was being unjust, and dynamite in bed.

She gave him a dark look. "What are you grinning at?"

"You're dynamite in bed. Do you know that?"

She made a face. "Is that relevant to this discussion?"

"I think so." His gaze fell to her lips and stayed there.

"How?"

"It has to do with our relationship," he said, but his voice was lower, almost distracted as his eyes traced the shape of her mouth. "You turn me on even when you're telling me off. How can that happen?"

A slow warmth was starting to seep through her. "Maybe because what I say is the truth, and because an honest woman turns you on."

"I doubt it. I think it's because you're such a little thing, and when you get up on your soapbox your cheeks turn pink and your eyes flash, your lips caress the words and your breasts go up and down with each breath. I'm a breast man."

"Do tell."

"I'd rather show." But it was her chin that he took in his fingers, and her mouth that he seized. His kiss was long and thorough. When he let her up for air, he said against her mouth, "So you really think I should go to Chicago?"

Her voice was a wisp of air. "Think? How can I think anything when you kiss me that way?"

"You said I should go to Chicago. I want you to come."

Her head cleared a little. "To Chicago?"

"To Chicago." He gave her another long, drugging kiss. "Or else I might change my mind halfway there. You're my conscience."

"I thought," she whispered, "I was dynamite in bed." Her eyes were heavy-lidded, her head back, her lips moist and parted.

Unable to resist their lure, he kissed her again, and this time he couldn't stop. His hands got into the act; his whole body got into the act. In no time, it seemed, clothes were strewn around the room, and they were making love on the plush dove-grey carpet. At one point Lily thought she heard him murmur, "I need you with me," but, if so, the words were overshadowed by deeds, and she lost all but the moment.

There was, of course, no question but that she'd go to Chicago with him. She loved him. As improbable as it seemed, when a week before she hadn't known he existed, she'd fallen hard. While her feelings for Jarrod had been conscious and rational, what she felt for Quist was more passionate on every count. It wasn't necessarily wise; she had no idea where it would lead, but it was strong enough to keep her from turning away. She was happy. Traveling with Quist, spending days and nights with him gave her pleasure. She had a right to that, she reasoned.

Quist was strong, perhaps headstrong at times, but gentle and caring as well. As angry as he might be at the fates, he couldn't sustain anger against her. Looking back on it, she realized he'd never been able to do it. Even at the beginning, he'd been more bark than bite. He made her feel protected; more than that, he made her feel worthy of his protection.

And he was good with Nicki. Lily loved the way he held the baby, careful but now steady and competently. Despite all his grumbling at the start, he seemed genuinely attached to Nicki. He didn't shy from carrying her, bathing her, even changing her diapers, and Lily suspected that if there was food to be spooned in, he'd do that, too. She wanted to believe that having Nicki and her in his life meant something special to him, and though he hadn't said as much in words, nothing of his actions suggested differently. After all, he could have been free of them in Quebec, but he was insisting they continue on with him to Chicago.

So she was going. Quebec held nothing special for her. She'd chosen it because it was new, because she'd heard good things about it, and because it was a safe distance from

Hartford and the long arm of Jarrod's family. The irony that she'd met Quist because his half sister had chosen to run there, too, didn't escape her. But she didn't dwell on it. Nor did she dwell on—or Quist raise the issue of—if, when and how she'd return to Quebec. She was taking one day at a time.

That seemed to be what Quist was doing, too. Though he kept a steady pace, he didn't break any speed records on the way to Chicago. He was keeping in daily touch with the ranch, though, enough to know that snow had fallen there, too. If there was more, he told Lily, and if the temperatures fell much, he was going to have to airlift hay to large numbers of his herd. He had to get back soon, he knew. Still, he wasn't racing.

Chicago was their crossroads. Though neither of them said as much, both knew that there were decisions to be made there. It was one thing to leave Quebec and head for another way station, but once they left Chicago—and Quist swore he wouldn't, couldn't go any farther in search of Jennifer—the next stop would be Montana. Lily's going there was a step that would take some discussion.

The discussion, though, once they reached Chicago, revolved around Jennifer. Reaching the city in the middle of the afternoon, they drove directly to the address Quist had been given. It was a small house on the outskirts of the city, modest verging on shabby. Lily was surprised. With the jumping from large city to large city that Jennifer had done, she'd expected something more cosmopolitan.

"They've all been places like this," Quist told her as he studied the house. "Very plain." He looked at Lily. "I'll go see if she's here. If she is, I'll be back for you." To the objective observer, he looked perfectly calm, but Lily had spent long enough studying his face to recognize the subtle tightness around his nose and mouth.

"Won't you want to see her yourself?" she asked. "Nicki and I can wait here."

"In the cold, no way. If I go in, you go in." He paused. "Aren't you a little bit curious?"

She gave him a crooked smile. "I suppose." She offered her mouth when he leaned over in search of it, then she watched him unfold his tall frame from the car and approach the house.

Two minutes later he came back for her. The tension remained around his nose and mouth, and Lily could have sworn she saw something approaching fear in his eyes. But it was gone before she could be sure, and after he helped her out, he took Nicki in his arms.

It occurred to Lily then that she and Nicki were Quist's security. They were his family as he confronted someone who was also his family but in whom he had no faith at all. Lily knew that she was a calming force for him; she'd seen it different times when he'd been tense or angry, when looking at her or touching her had relaxed him. The situation with Jennifer clearly put him on edge. It also opened up feelings of vulnerability. If Lily gave him confidence, that was good. She found deep satisfaction in being there for him.

Jennifer Simmons had no one to give her confidence. Her vulnerability was right there on the surface, along with features that were young and lovely and eyes that were years too old. She was dressed simply, in jeans and a shirt, and she looked up at Quist as though she didn't know whether to hug him or run away.

Awkwardly she introduced them to the older woman with whom she was staying, and showed them into the house. When they were seated in the living room, she swallowed hard. She looked down at her hands, which were pale and tightly clenched. She looked up at Quist.

"Thank you for coming," she said in an unsteady voice. "I wasn't sure you'd follow me here."

Quist wanted to be angry with her. She was his mother's daughter, and he'd been angry at his mother all his life. But at first glance Jennifer looked more unwitting than evil. So rather than be angry, he was cautious. "You gave my name to your friends. I assumed you expected me."

She shook her head. Her hair was dark like Quist's but shorter and fine. It hugged her head and would have made her look waiflike if she hadn't been so tall. Lily guessed her to be five nine. She also guessed that she could have been a model if she'd wanted to.

"I didn't know what to expect," Jennifer said, still unsteadily, "but I had nowhere else to turn."

Where else but to blood kin, Lily thought as dozens of questions flooded into her mind. If she'd been Quist, she'd have been wondering whether Jennifer looked like her mother, whether they'd been close, what her mother had been like, whether Jennifer had any other siblings, whether her mother had remarried and finally settled down, whether she'd ever mentioned Quist.

Quist wasn't unaware of those questions. But he was guarded, not yet ready to open up that part of the relationship. "You told me there was a man, that he was involved in embezzlement and that he planned to implicate you in it."

Jennifer held herself straight, but there was a fine trembling in her arms that made her shirt shimmer as though there was a wind whispering through the weave. She hesitated for just a minute, seeming as reluctant to trust Quist as he was to trust her. Then a tiny flicker of resignation crossed her features, suggesting that she had no choice.

"His name is Walker Keane. I've known him most of my life, but it's just been the last two years that we've been together."

"You're having an affair with him?" Quist asked bluntly.

She looked down. "Yes. We—I thought he was a good person. He had a nice place to live, and he was always buying me things. All he asked was that I look good for him. He liked to show me off. I made him feel younger."

That sounded ominous. "How old is he?"

"Forty-three."

Quist was silent, trying to reconcile the twenty-four-year difference in ages. He thought of Lily's being eleven years younger than him, but eleven years wasn't twenty-four.

Jennifer made no attempt to rationalize the difference. If anything, she seemed eager to get away from it. "We were living in Albany. He was a free-lance business manager. He would hire himself out to different companies for a limited period of time. That meant he could work as much or as little as he wanted to, and it meant that we could go away a lot. He liked doing that, going off on trips."

"Did you?"

She hesitated, then nodded. "Walker's the only man I've ever really known. I trusted him. From the first I can remember, he was always around, and even though he used to get into some awful battles with Mom—"

"He's been around that long?"

"Since I was seven or eight."

The guy sounded perverse to Quist. "He was attracted to you back then?"

"Not to me," Jennifer said. "To Mom."

Nicki started crying. Only after Quist handed her over to Lily did he realize how tightly he'd been holding her. With a determined effort, he relaxed his muscles.

But Jennifer was leaning forward, smiling at Nicki in a way that made the girl look fifteen. "She's adorable. How old is she?"

"Almost six weeks now," Lily said.

Jennifer's gaze skipped back and forth from Nicki's face to Lily's, then Quist's. "She looks like you," she told Lily, and Lily didn't say a word as to why that should be so.

Neither did Quist, but only in part because he didn't mind being mistaken for Nicki's father. The other part was still trying to comprehend what Jennifer had said about her mother and Walker Keane. It disgusted him to think that mother and daughter had been involved with the same man, even if it had been at different times.

"How did Keane get into trouble?" he asked a bit sharply.

Jennifer looked up from Nicki, and her smile quickly faded. "I'm not sure how or when it started. All I know is that he's been accused of stealing hundreds of thousands of dollars from different ones of the companies he worked for."

"Where do you come in?"

"He doesn't have much of a defense, I guess, so he's going to say that I put him up to it."

"A nineteen-year-old girl?" Quist asked skeptically.

"And before me, my mother. He'll say that the original scheme was hers, and that I just carried on after she died."

"Does he have proof?"

"How can he have proof if it's not true?" she cried. It was the first time she'd betrayed any of the frustration she was feeling, but she quickly regained control of herself. "He has proof that we helped him spend the money, and we did that, only we thought he'd come by it honestly."

"Your mother cared about things like honesty?" Quist blurted out. He couldn't control the asking any more than he could the bitterness behind it.

Jennifer remained quiet, thinking, choosing her words. "I know you have no reason to feel anything for her. She wasn't much of a mother to you."

"Much?" he echoed tartly.

"Okay, she wasn't a mother at all," Jennifer said, and both her tone and her look said that her guard was down. "But she was to me. She never got divorced from your father, so she never married mine, and he didn't stick around long enough for it to matter. So I grew up with one parent, too, except that after a little bit we had Walker. But the whole time, Mom tried. She worked as a bookkeeper until Walker said she didn't have to work anymore, and I was glad he said it. She worked too hard. She worked too hard trying to be good with Walker, too. Sometimes she was his mother and sometimes his lover, and sometimes she was something in between. That was when there was trouble. But all she wanted was to have us be together, Walker and me and her. Maybe she felt she'd blown it once—I don't know, because she never mentioned you to me, but I do know that she liked the idea of family."

She stopped and was studying Quist. "You're older than I thought you'd be."

"She was seventeen when I was born."

"Maybe she was too young to handle having a baby. Did she love your father?"

"I doubt it."

"Do you remember her at all?"

"No. I was an infant when she left."

Jennifer frowned and looked away. "I wonder what she did all those years in between." She looked back up at Quist. "What do you think? She never talked about the past. It was like her life began when I was born. When I used to ask her questions about where she was born or what it was like when she was little, she'd give me general answers that said nothing at all."

Quist wanted to offer some kind of dark speculation as to what the woman had done after she'd abandoned his father and him, and though he had plenty of words at the ready, he couldn't get himself to utter a one. He was coming to wonder whether Jennifer Simmons wasn't, in her way, a victim of her mother, too. Jennifer had loved the woman. He couldn't see deliberately hurting her for the sake of his own vengeance. Far safer to stick to Jennifer's present predicament.

So he cleared his throat. "Where is Keane now?"

"In Albany."

"Has he been indicted?"

She nodded. "He's out on bail."

"And he actually told you what he planned?"

"He was drunk, but he didn't deny it when I pinned him down the next day."

"So you ran?"

"As fast as I could. I went to stay with someone in Albany, but he came for me there. I thought I could lose him in Manhattan, but I got a call saying he was on his way."

"Who are the people you've been staying with?"

"Friends of my mother. We used to visit them a lot when I was little but not so much after we moved in with Walker. I was counting on their loyalty lying with me."

Quist was grateful she'd had that much sense. She'd been pretty dumb carrying on with a hand-me-down from her mother, but then, she was young, seventeen at the time she'd started in with Keane. Seventeen was the same age his mother had been when she had him and left. And at seventeen, he'd been no cherub, himself. Maybe bad judgment at that age ran in the family.

But that was as far as he wanted to go with family analyses. "What do you want from me?" he asked. It didn't matter that he felt an unbidden affinity for the girl; he wasn't about to be used without knowing the score.

"Advice." She looked at him straight on and would have conveyed utter confidence if it hadn't been for that same fine trembling in her arms. "I think I need a lawyer, but I don't know the first thing about how to go about getting one who would be good for something like this. I tried to reach Henry Melnick—he was the lawyer who called me after my mother died and told me about you—but he's dead, and I don't know where else to turn. My mother's friends—the people I've stayed with—don't know. Walker was in control of just about my whole life." Looking off to the side, she said more quietly, "I don't have much money, and I can't get a loan from the bank." She looked back at him with as determined a gaze as he'd received from her. "But I'll pay you back. I'll work for you, or work somewhere else and make payments to you every week from my salary. I can type, or file, or do whatever somebody trains me to do. But I don't want to go to jail."

The silence that followed her words was abrupt and final, indeed like the steel doors of a prison clanging shut.

Quist continued to study her, but Lily's words were the ones echoing in his mind. *Can you really go home and forget about her? Won't you feel guilty? You'll always wonder.*

"You won't go to jail," he said at last.

"If Walker implicates me, I will."

"He's only using you to take a little of the weight off him. No prosecutor will charge you without solid evidence." He truly believed that, but he had no intention of leaving it to chance. Rising from the sofa, he reached down to take Nicki from Lily. "There's a lawyer I trust in Billings. He won't handle the case himself, but he'll give us the name of someone in New York who can."

With Lily at his side, he went to the door. There, he turned back to Jennifer, who was standing in the hall looking nearly as unsure as she had at the first.

"I'll make the calls from the hotel. We'll be staying at the Hyatt. If you want to join us there for dinner, I may have something to tell you. Say, eight?"

Jennifer nodded.

Only after they were back in the car and stuck in the rush-hour traffic did Lily turn to Quist. "What do you think?" she asked cautiously. He'd been looking dark since they'd left the house.

He shrugged.

"Is that a 'she's nice'?"

"It's a 'she's young and lost and I don't know what the hell else, because I barely spent twenty minutes with the girl.'"

"You liked her."

"I didn't spend *long* enough with her to like her."

"But you'll help her."

"A few calls. I'm making a few calls, and I'll pick up the tab, but only because I have the money and I got nothing better to do with it. And, anyway, she'll pay me back."

Lily doubted he'd make her do that, but she said nothing. Well, almost nothing. "You and Jennifer have the same nose."

There was dead silence for a minute, then a rather annoyed, "So?"

"Just making an observation."

Quist made the same observation that night at dinner. Shortly afterward, he gave Jennifer the name, address and phone number of a top-notch lawyer in New York who was expecting to hear from her the next day. He also gave her an airline ticket, plus a check made out to the lawyer. "This will more than cover his retainer. He's to put the excess in an account for your use. I want you to stay in New York until he tells you you can leave. Keep in close touch with him, and whatever you do, don't go running off. This lawyer is your ticket to freedom from Keane."

Jennifer's gratitude was written all over her face. She looked as if she would have thrown her arms around him if he'd shown the slightest receptiveness to that. But he didn't. And though Lily, who knew how warm and physical Quist could be, could have kicked him for keeping his distance, she understood that he needed time.

For Lily, though, time was running out. She had to know where she was going, whether it would be back to Quebec or on to Quist's ranch. The issue weighed heavily on her mind when they returned to their room, and once Nicki had been put to bed, she couldn't put it off any longer.

"Quist?"

He'd just put down the phone from talking with his foreman, but his eyes had been on her the whole time. "Mmm?"

There was a different intonation to his hum. She had a strong suspicion he was thinking the same thing she was. So without preamble, she asked, "What now?"

His eyes dropped to her shoulders, then her breasts, and he invited her over with a toss of his head. Always pleased to be close to him, she rounded the bed and slipped under the arm he offered. He didn't speak, though, but put his lips against her hair.

"Quist?"

"I'm thinking."

"You have to go home."

"I know."

"Maybe I should be heading back to Quebec."

"You can't drive."

"Why not?"

"Alone in the car for that distance with Nicki, it's too much. Maybe if your wrist wasn't broken."

"My wrist is okay. It just aches once in a while. I can do most everything with the cast on."

"You shouldn't do much."

"I have to. I have to get on with my life, Quist."

He didn't say anything, but she could feel the acceleration of his pulse. Taking her face in the V of his hand, he tipped it up. "Kiss me," he ordered and took her lips hard.

She kissed him, loving the hardness for the passion it contained. He was a hard-driving man with a good heart. She wanted to be the one who gave that heart a workout. But his kiss went on, filling her senses, increasingly, to the exclusion of all else.

"Quist, wait," she whispered once, but he didn't allow her any other words. He kept her mouth busy with his own, and by the time he moved on to other parts of her body, she wasn't thinking of talk. Before long they were naked and in bed, writhing against each other in a timeless drive toward release, and when it came, it was better than it had ever been before.

Which was precisely what she'd thought the last time they'd made love, and the time before that, and the time before that.

I love you, she wanted to say, but she didn't dare. What she did say, when they'd regained their senses, pulled up the blanket and relaxed comfortably against each other was, "We have to talk, Quist."

"No need," he murmured sleepily. "You're coming to Montana. This is too good to give up."

"This . . . what?" she asked.

"What we have.

"What's that?"

"Something good."

"Something good in bed?"

"That, too."

She watched him closely, looked at the way his eyelids lay perfectly at rest and the way the muscles of his face were calm and the way his chest expanded with each slow, sleepy breath he took. And while she wished he was wide awake, looking her in the eye and telling her that he loved her, she had a suspicion that just then, warm and spent and unguarded as he was, he had come as close to that admission as he could.

Forty years of resistance wasn't about to topple in a few short days. Loving Quist, knowing that she wanted to be with him, Lily figured that she could give it a little longer.

9

AFTER FOUR MONTHS of living with Quist, Lily didn't regret her decision. She loved the ranch. That wasn't to say that she'd loved it from the start. It had looked big, barren and cold when she'd first seen it in January. Very much the city girl Quist had accused her of being, she was overwhelmed by the expanse of snow-covered prairie and the harshness of the hills, by the distance the ranch was from others, by the pervasive darkness of the night. More than once she pined for the noise and lights of the city.

She didn't tell Quist that. She didn't want him to think she couldn't hack it, when she knew she could. Okay, so the land was large and foreign. So she felt more comfortable inside the house and most comfortable when Quist was with her. Everything was new. She was flexible. She could adapt.

She did. As the days passed, she got used to the largeness of things. She realized that she wouldn't be swallowed up by the land if she went out for a walk with Nicki. Nor would she meet a bear. Nor would a catastrophe happen with no one around to help. If anything, *because* there were fewer people around, those people were more attentive.

The ranch house itself was a pleasure. A single-story, sprawling structure, it blended into the prairie with far more charm that she'd expected to find in Montana. Quist had been right about creature comforts. While she wouldn't have called the house plush, it had all the modern amenities she could want. And once she'd softened the rooms with things like plants, decorative baskets and wall hangings, she felt very much at home.

Yes, she loved the ranch, but mostly she loved what she did there. Her days were filled with taking care of Nicki, polishing the handsome oak furniture, baking things like cinnamon-raisin bread, fresh carrot muffins and Swedish apple pie—and her nights were filled with Quist, which was the icing on the cake.

Her wrist had healed well and was long since forgotten. With the gradual onset of spring, she thrived. Nicki thrived, too. Quist had found a pediatrician they both liked, and one glowing report after another came each month. Still a baby but looking more like a little girl each day, Nicki had the kind of sunny temperament that brought smiles to the faces of those around her, and that included the ranch hands, whom she charmed to a man.

Quist was the most charmed. He never made a big thing of it in front of Lily, but time and again she would find him in a quiet corner playing with Nicki. He always checked on her before he went to bed, and looked in on her again when he awoke at dawn. In turn, Nicki came alive when he entered the room, and when he came close, she raised her arms to him in a bid to be held.

There were times when Lily grew teary-eyed watching the two of them together. She loved Quist for adoring Nicki and loved Nicki for adoring Quist. Each blossomed under the other's attention. Their relationship was innocent and sweet.

But there were times—granted not often, because Lily did everything she could not to think about it—when she grew teary-eyed wishing the relationship were more. Though he fit the role well, Quist wasn't her husband. Nor was he Nicki's father. Lily didn't know what Nicki would call Quist when she started to talk, or how she'd explain his position

in her life to little friends when she went off to school.
Something had to happen before then, Lily knew, but she
couldn't push the issue.

She was too happy to risk that. It sometimes frightened
her to think that if she'd stayed in Hartford a day longer, or
taken early shelter from the storm in a motel, or taken a
different road or even the same road at a different time, she'd
have missed Quist. As unlikely as any relationship between them had seemed back then, she couldn't imagine life
without him. He filled every one of her needs. Even after
four months together, her pulses raced when he came near.
After that length of time, any critic who would have attri-
buted their relationship to the experience of being snowbound together had to be silenced.

To Lily's knowledge, though, there weren't any critics.
Quist had friends and acquaintances at neighboring ranches
and in town, and they welcomed her warmly. Several of his
ranch hands went so far as to say that Quist's disposition
had taken an upswing since she'd come, and though one
part of her wondered whether they weren't just buttering her
up for the sake of the mocha-nut cake she made, which they
loved, the other part of her accepted their compliment with
pride.

There was one critic, though. Like a bad dream, she'd
thought of him from time to time since she'd come to live
with Quist. But Quist made her feel safe and protected, and
Montana was a long way from Connecticut. It wasn't Jarrod; he had remarried and would do, she knew, everything
he could to forget that Lily existed. It was Michael. She
hadn't dreamed that he would follow her.

He did just that. Late one Monday morning in the beginning of June, he showed up at the door. Unsuspecting, she
went to answer his knock. She was wearing jeans and a
shirt, and was wiping her hands of remnants of the bread

dough she'd just put in the oven. She came to an abrupt halt several steps from the screen when she saw who was there.

Her first thought was to look around for help, but she controlled the urge. "Michael," she said with cool civility.

He dipped his head in greeting. His blond hair was as perfectly groomed as always, his skin as perfectly tanned, his slacks and cotton sweater as perfectly chic. With all that perfection, he looked distinctly out of place. "Aren't you going to let me in?"

"That depends." She resumed wiping her hands on the dish towel. "What do you want?"

"To talk."

"About what?"

"What you've done with yourself in the past few months."

"I don't see why that should be of any interest to you," she said, and though she'd tried to say it evenly, something of her inner feeling must have come through. The battle lines were drawn.

Without invitation, Michael opened the screen and stepped inside. Lily countered by quickly sidestepping him, hooking the towel on the coatrack and escaping to the porch he'd just left.

"D.J.!" she bellowed at the top of her lungs. "D.J.!"

"What in the hell are you doing?" Michael cried, holding the screen door open. "I just want to talk."

She drilled him with a look. "Last time you said that, you ended up throwing things at me." She looked back at the barn in time to see a young man striding purposefully toward her. "I've learned not to make the same mistake twice," she added, then called to D.J., "Can I have your help for a minute? This man wants to talk with me, but I don't care to be alone with him."

"Sure thing, ma'am," D. J. said with a drawl and a smile. He took the two front steps in one stride, then posted himself against the porch rail.

Michael should have been humiliated, but he wasn't. Not Michael. He stared at the young man for a long minute before turning to Lily. "You're a coward."

"Uh-huh." She felt better now that D.J. was there, but that didn't mean she was calm. Her insides shook. She wished she were five ten and robust. She wished she wore armor. She wished Quist were around, but he was out in the Jeep. "So, what do you want?"

Again Michael looked at D.J., but the younger man showed no sign either of looking away or leaving. Finally he decided to ignore him, and, in a pleasant voice, asked Lily, "How have you been?"

"Just fine."

"You're seeing something of the country, I take it." When she didn't respond to that, he smiled and asked, "Do you miss the east yet?"

"Not really."

"This is . . . different."

"Uh-huh."

He looked off toward the barn, then the open range, then back toward the inside of the house. "A rancher's mistress. Funny, I hadn't pegged you for the mistress type."

Lily felt a momentary chill, but she shook it off. "Wasn't that what you had in mind for me back in Hartford?"

"Of course not. I wanted to marry you."

She'd never heard anything as absurd, but it didn't seem worth her breath to tell him so. "What are you here for, Michael?"

"You," he said. When she gave him a you-must-be-crazy look, he insisted, "I want you to come back with me."

"Why would I want to do that?" she asked in disbelief.

"Because you and I could be good together."

"I don't believe this," she murmured. She turned her head toward D.J. "I don't *believe* this." She glared back at Michael. "Last time you were threatening me with all kinds of ugly things, and that was before you got violent."

"I was upset. I said things I shouldn't have."

"You certainly did, but that's not even the issue. The issue is that there's nothing between us. There's never *been* anything between us, despite what you threatened to say. Why on earth would I want to go back east with you?"

"Because this is no way to live." He shot a disparaging glance around. "Animals live on places like this. People choose more cultured surroundings."

Even aside from the fact that he'd just insulted D.J., who was within earshot, and Quist and all the others, who weren't, Lily felt personally offended. After all, she'd chosen to live on the ranch. She could have left at any time. "I think you'd better go."

"After I've come all this way to see you?"

That raised another issue, one she wanted answered out of sheer curiosity. "How did you find me?"

But Michael was looking at the approaching ribbon of dust. "Is that your rancher?"

Lily was relieved that it was. She was also relieved that D.J. didn't move. "How did you find me?"

"You wired the bank to have your account transferred here. Where's Nicole?"

The chill she felt this time wasn't so easily shaken off, and at the back of her eyes, she felt the prick of tears. "Nicole is none of your affair," she said on a note of warning.

"She's my niece."

Lily held herself still. "I have a paper that waives any claim you or your family may have on her."

"I'm saying that I care. How is she?" When Lily remained stone-faced, he said, "She was very little when I saw her last. I'll bet she's grown."

Lily refused to even acknowledge Nicki's presence, though she was, at that moment, close by, in a wind-up swing in the kitchen.

"Come on, Lily. I'm her uncle. I'm curious."

"Nicki and I are doing just fine. Now that you know that, and now that you know I won't go back east with you, you can leave."

"You really intend to raise her here?"

Lily didn't blink. "You can leave, Michael." She didn't want him there. His presence was contaminating something that was good and pure and healthy.

"For God's sake, what kind of a life is this for a child? I mean, if you want to play the rancher's maid, that's one thing. But think of Nicole. She shouldn't have to live this way."

"Live what way?" Lily demanded, trembling now with anger and doing little to hide it.

"A bare-bones existence. This isn't life. It's just survival. Where do you go to shop around here? Where do you go to eat out? No theater? No symphony? The two of you could be spending your days at the club. Nicole could be seeing other children like her, instead of groveling with cows and dust and people who probably haven't graduated from high school."

Lily was livid. "Are you saying that a diploma is a sign of intelligence? That, Michael, is probably one of the most ignorant comments I've ever heard."

"You know what I mean."

"No, I don't. The people I've met here are open and intelligent, and when it comes to common sense, or perceptiveness, or sensitivity, they're head and shoulders above you and Jarrod—*combined*. 'I should be at the club,'" she mimicked. "I *hated* the club. When I think back to the people I met through you two, I thank God Nicki's not there. I'd rather have my daughter growing up knowing people like D.J. any day."

Michael's mouth twisted as he shot a derisive glance at the young cowhand. "Are you putting out for him, too?"

Tears gathered on her lower lids. She was rigid with fury. "Leave, Michael."

But instead of leaving, he narrowed his eyes. "Think, Lily. Think back to when you conceived Nicole and all the things you wanted for her then. This isn't for you, and it's not for her." He darted a glance at the Jeep, which had reached the driveway to the house. "And what kind of relationship do you have with that guy, anyway?" He grabbed her hand, ignoring D.J., who had remained immobile in the face of personal insults but now immediately straightened. "No wedding band. He hasn't married you. You've been living here servicing him all this time, and he hasn't married you? That's dumb, Lily. Really dumb. Oh, not on his part. I have to give him credit for that. He knows a good thing when he sees one. He's got a cook, a laundress, a housekeeper and a lover all for free. What kind of woman is going to put up with that bull?"

Lily yanked her hand back. "No bull, and I know what it looks like, because you and Jarrod gave me plenty. Everything I have here is good. I've never been happier." She heard the Jeep pull to a halt not far from the steps.

"And you think it'll last?" Michael asked, but his words were lower and coming quickly, as though he knew that he was running out of time. "You think he'll still want you in a year, or two or three? He'll tire of you. Or Nicole. Wait till she gets bigger and starts making demands. You think he's going to want you then? You'll be out in the cold, Lily. Out . . . in . . . the . . . cold."

"What's going on here?" Quist asked. His voice was deep and steel-edged, and his eyes were on Michael as he put a possessive arm around Lily's shoulder.

"This," Lily said shakily, "is Michael, my former brother-in-law. I told you about him. Do you remember?"

Quist certainly did. He remembered everything Lily had said and the way she'd said it. "What's he doing here?"

"He came to see how I was. But he's just leaving. Weren't you, Michael?"

The expression on Michael's perfectly tanned face suggested he was feeling thwarted, but he didn't let on to it in words. And Lily could understand why. Michael was tall, but Quist was taller. Quist was also broader and more heavily muscled, a fact that was made abundantly clear by the snug fit of his chambray shirt across his chest and the sinewy forearms that extended beyond the roll of his sleeves.

Michael recognized a formidable opponent when he saw one. Without saying a thing, he sent a final hard look at Lily. Then, exhibiting perfect posture to match his perfect attire, he walked past her, down the steps and to his car.

Quist went after him.

"Wait, Quist," Lily cautioned.

He held up a hand to reassure her, but he didn't look back. Lily watched apprehensively while he leaned low at the driver's window. She couldn't hear what he said. The distance was a little too far, his voice a little too low, the breeze a little too active in the grasses beyond the barn. The instant he straightened, Michael's car shot forward.

"I'll be goin' back to work now, ma'am," D.J. said.

Lily had momentarily forgotten his presence. At the sound of his voice, she swung a surprised look his way. "Uh, oh, sure, D.J. And thanks. Thanks for being here." Softly, just a hair above a whisper, she added, "Please forget what you heard. I don't want to upset Quist."

"Sure thing, ma'am," he said, and with a tip of his hat, he was gone.

Seconds later Quist came up the steps, but Lily was already on her way inside. Heart thudding, she made straight for the kitchen. Nicki was in the swing, just where she'd been left. Its wind-up had long since wound down, but she was perfectly content gnawing on one of the rubber teethers Lily had tied with a ribbon to the chain of the swing.

At sight of her mother, she began to gurgle and grin. Lifting her, Lily held her tightly, closed her eyes and swayed gently from side to side.

"Lily?" Quist came forward from the open archway.

"I'm okay," she breathed.

"You're shaking like a leaf. Did he threaten you again?"

"No. Seeing him was bad enough."

Babbling, Nicki began to kick against Lily's waist.

"He won't be back."

She opened her eyes. "What did you say to him?"

Quist wasn't going to tell her, because it was too crude. "Let's just say I made a little threat of my own. I think he understands that I'll carry it out if he comes near you again."

Again. Did that mean *ever* again, as in during the course of her lifetime? She couldn't ask, couldn't push.

"Hi, pumpkin," Quist said softly to Nicki. When she held out an arm, he took her gently in his. "How long was he here?" he asked Lily.

"Not long. Just a few minutes."

"Did he ask to see Nicki?"

"No. He asked how she was. That's all."

Quist wanted to know what they'd talked about, but he didn't ask. Sounding insecure, which perhaps he was, wasn't part of his image. Sounding distrustful, which perhaps had been true at one point, was no longer. He did trust Lily. He knew that her feelings for him were strong. He couldn't see her picking up and leaving him.

He figured that in her own good time, she'd tell him what Michael had said.

Unfortunately she didn't, and it would have been all right, if they'd settled back into their lives without any sign of the slightest disturbance. But Lily seemed to be quieter at times, not quite preoccupied, not quite as carefree in her silence as she'd been. It didn't happen often, but Quist was so keenly attuned to her that he noticed whenever it did. When he asked if something was bothering her, she put on her brightest smile and assured him nothing was, and then she'd be her usual self for a while, as though she was making a concerted effort not to let him see. He began to wonder how much time she spent when he was gone, thinking about whatever it was.

A few minutes; that was all the time she'd spent with Michael, but he'd said something that lingered. Quist knew it, and the longer he wondered what it was, the more unsure he grew. The wondering was like a chisel, chipping away at the fragile base of his trust.

In his mind, the issue was a simple one. He wanted Lily to stay with him. He feared that Michael had made her a counteroffer, and while he didn't believe that she'd seriously consider accepting, knowing how she felt about Michael, he couldn't help but wonder if she was rethinking her position in his life.

He wanted to ask her, but he couldn't seem to find the words. Actually he couldn't seem to find the courage. He didn't know what he'd do if she told him that yes, she was rethinking things.

In the end the words he found surprised even him, though the time and place didn't. They'd just made love on the charcoal-gray sheets on his king-size bed. It had been a hard, fiery coupling that had carried them long and far. Their bodies were slick with sweat and exhausted. As always at times like those, Quist's guard was down.

"Marry me, Lily," he said.

Lily didn't move for a minute. Her heart, which had just settled into a relatively even beat, began to pound again. She wondered if she'd heard wrong, or if she'd imagined the words because she'd wanted to hear them so badly. Levering herself up, she looked into his face. It was damp and slumberous, but his eyes were open and though he seemed a little unbalanced, he was looking straight at her.

"Well?" he prodded.

"Uh, what—will you say that again?"

"I want you to marry me."

She was ecstatic—and frightened. Tears came to her eyes, but she willed them back. "Why?"

"Because I like the life we have together. I think it should be formalized."

That wasn't what she wanted to hear. "Why formalized?"

"I don't know. It just seems right. We're living as husband and wife. Why not make it official?"

"Is that what you really want?" she asked warily.

Quist had been hoping for a warmer reception. He wondered if his fears were founded, after all. The thought of that made him more uneasy than ever. "I want to know you won't leave."

"I won't leave."

"Then marry me."

Lily studied his face for a minute, studied the firm set of his jaw, the straight line of his mouth, the dark eyes that were more enigmatic than they'd been in a while, and though she wanted to melt into him, say yes and make him happy, her own happiness rested on knowing more. She couldn't go through life wondering whether Michael's visit had prompted the proposal. "Why now?"

"Because it's time, don't you think?" He scowled for a minute, wishing he had more patience, but when it came to matters of the heart he was too much a novice to feint and parry. Taking her face a little roughly in his hands, he said, "I'd make you a good husband. I'd make Nicki a good father. I want to have more kids, and you do, too, but I won't do that unless we're married."

Lily loved everything he was saying, still he hadn't told her what she needed to know. So she argued, "Not so long ago, you didn't like women. You weren't interested in marriage."

"I've changed."

"Just like that?"

"No, not 'just like that.'" His hands gentled around her face, thumbs picking up the long teardrops that seemed suspended at the corners of her eyes. "It's been six months, and I fought it at first. One part of me still fights—old habits die hard—but I don't want to go back to the other way of living." When she still looked skeptical, he said, "I've been good with Jennifer, haven't I?"

Lily was the first to admit that he had. He'd kept in close touch with the lawyer from New York, and Jennifer had even been west for a visit, with another one planned for the fall. While there wasn't the kind of brother-sister closeness that came from siblings sharing a past, they had a start.

"You've been very good with her," Lily said. "But that's different. She's someone you can see or not, be close to or not. You don't pick your relatives, but you do pick your wife, and if you pick her for the wrong reasons—" She sat up, effectively removing her face from his hands. Perching sideways, she drew her knees to her chest for the warmth she missed.

Quist grew cautious. "What is it, Lily?" His voice was low and slow as he studied her profile. "You're thinking something—you've been thinking something for a while now, and I've been trying to figure out what it is, but I keep coming up with zip. Tell me. I need to know."

Lily stared at the needlepoint wall hanging she'd made for the room; it was burgundy and gray to match the sheets and spread, but the gray was pale and soft, far more feminine than charcoal. It was her personal stamp on this room that was masculine in so many other respects, and it was symbolic of all she'd tried to do in his life. *It's time, don't you think?* he'd asked her. She figured he was right. If he didn't love her now, he never would. It was time to be completely forthright.

"I've been thinking about lots of things," she began. "I suppose that Michael—"

"Michael," Quist cut in. The name brought him sharply to a sitting position. "I knew it had to do with him."

"But it doesn't," she argued, eyeing him over the edge of her shoulder. "Not really. But he voiced things I'd been thinking about for a while. It's one thing when they're in your own mind, another when someone who doesn't even think the way you do says them."

Quist accepted that. Bending a knee, he propped an elbow on it and tried to look casual. "So what did he say?"

"He talked about me as your mistress. He said you had a good thing going, with someone to cook and clean and do everything else around the house. He said you'd get tired of me—"

"No *way*—" Quist began, but Lily cut him off with a hand on his arm as she twisted to face him.

"I know," she said softly. Her throat felt tight, but she pushed the words past it. "I think I knew it a long time ago, because you seemed legitimately pleased to have me here. But there was always that little question in my mind about *why* you were pleased. There was always that little question about whether it was me you liked having around, or a live-in maid, cook, lover. I didn't think about it all the time. I really didn't think about it much. I tried *never* to think about it, but that didn't work, because I've been used—and abused—once, and the hurt is still fresh. Then Michael came, and suddenly it was like he took all my little fears and put them in lights."

"But I want to marry you," Quist insisted. "*You*. Not anyone else I've known in my life. *You*. I could have hired a live-in maid, if that was what I wanted. Or a cook. Or a lover. I've got the money. But I never wanted to have anyone around. Then I met you, and things changed."

"Things."

"What I wanted."

"Why?"

"What do you mean, why?"

"Why did things change? You'd been happy before. From what you said, you were perfectly content with your life."

Quist looked off to the side. "Yeah. That's what I said."

"Weren't you?"

He looked down, thoughtful as his eyes focused unseeingly on the rumpled sheets. "I suppose I was. I had a safe life. I wasn't taking any chances on women. I used them on my terms. I protected myself." He stopped. His gaze rose to the spot where the pale flesh of Lily's hip met the wrinkled sheet. "Then I met you. You were so damned honest, it was hard not to trust you. But there was something else. For the first time in my life, I was taking care of a woman."

He raised his eyes to find that hers had flooded. When he winced, she said quickly, "It's okay. I'm okay. Go on."

He stared at her long enough to make sure that the tears were staying put. Then he shrugged. "What's to say? I enjoyed taking care of you."

"You didn't feel you were being used?"

"How could I feel that, when you resisted my help, and then you were giving me back even more than I was giving." He scowled. "Damn it, Lily, what do you want me to say? I want you here. I want to go on taking care of you. I want to go on taking care of Nicki. I want us to spend the rest of our lives together."

"You could say that you love me," she blurted out, then quickly bit her lip. She hadn't wanted to say that. It was supposed to have come from him. She was about to say something to cover the gaffe when the look of incredulity on his face stopped her.

"Of course I love you," he cried in astonishment. "Isn't that what I've been saying? Isn't it what I've been *doing* for months?"

Tears shimmered in her eyes. "You never said it. I didn't know. You never said it. I need to hear the words."

Unable to hold himself apart from her any longer, he hooked an elbow around her neck and one around her waist and pulled her to him. He ducked his head, sliding his face against her hair. "I love you, Lily." He paused. "And I need to hear them, too."

"I love you," she said, letting the tears go at last.

He was holding her so tightly that it was a miracle she could move to breathe, much less cry, but she did the latter, with the smallest, softest sobs. "I hope it's happiness," he remarked against her cheek.

"And relief." She sniffled, cried a little more, then put her hand over the wet spot she'd made on his chest. The hair was matted; she rubbed it with her fingers, feeling the strength underneath. "I was so afraid. I tried not to be. I kept telling myself that you had to feel something for me, because you were so good to me, and you seemed so happy, but there was always this niggling little doubt."

She hurried on, ignoring the hiccoughing that broke the rush of her thoughts. "Then Michael started talking about the future and what kind of life I'd have here, and it made me realize even more how good it is. It's just the kind of life I want—I love it here, it suits who I am and who I want to be, *you* suit who I am and who I want to be." She took in a trembling breath. "But then I started thinking about what would happen if I ever lost you or lost what I have here." She looked up at him with eyes that were large, still damp but true windows to her soul. "I don't want that to happen, Quist."

For a minute Quist couldn't say a word. He was wondering what he'd ever done to deserve the woman he held in his arms. She was warm and giving, honest, strong enough to support him, vulnerable enough to need his support. And she did love him. It was there in her eyes, spilling from her soul. He'd seen it before, though he'd never had the courage to call it what it was for fear of losing it, but never before had he seen it in quite such a raw state. If he'd doubted before, he no longer did. Lily's love was a part of her being. She could no more free herself from it than she could do without a heart.

That was pretty much the way he felt, he realized. A future without Lily was no future at all. She gave his life dimension, depth and color. His love for her was boundless.

"So," he said a little hoarsely, "will you marry me?"

"Oh, yes," she whispered and offered her lips for a kiss to seal the vow.

Epilogue

LILY COULD LOOK at him for hours, which was very much what she did during the first day of his life. She put him to her breast, but her milk hadn't come in yet, and still she found pleasure from his sucking.

Though he was sleeping quietly now, he had a strong pair of lungs. He was also long and had a shock of dark hair so like his father's that Lily grinned through her tears each time she combed it with her fingers.

He was a beautiful baby. Nicole had been beautiful, too, and still was. Inside and out. Lily was blessed.

"Anybody sleeping?" came a deep-murmured call from the door.

She looked up to see two faces peering around the door's edge. Quist was clearly making a game of it, with Nicki not quite sure she wanted to play. It was the first time she'd seen her mother since Lily had gone into labor. It was also the first time she'd been in a hospital since her own birth, and she looked apprehensive.

At the sight of them, Lily's throat went tight. But she smiled broadly, held out her free arm and wiggled her fingers in invitation. Quist brought Nicki into the room. She was clinging to his neck, pressing her cheek to his shoulder, peering at Lily as though she didn't want to, but couldn't resist.

"Hi, sweetheart," Lily finally said. "You look so pretty. Daddy put on your favorite dress?" It was lime-green gingham with grosgrain ribbon at the bodice and hem, and beneath it were white tights and tiny white strap shoes. "And he put a ribbon in your hair." Which was shoulder length, light brown and shiny. "You're my gorgeous little girl." Lily held out her arm. "Can I have a hug, gorgeous little girl?"

But Nicki tightened her arms around Quist's neck and turned her face into his shoulder.

"No hug for Mommy?" Quist asked softly. When she shook her head, he said, "Well, I want to give her one. She's my favorite big girl." He bent over and gave Lily an eloquent kiss, then sat down on the edge of the bed.

"You said *I* was your favorite big girl," came the tiny voice from his shoulder. For a three-year-old, Nicki was unusually verbal. But then, Lily mused, she was unusual in lots of ways.

Quist's eyes smiled at Lily over Nicki's head. "You're right. You are my favorite big girl. Mommy's my favorite *big* big girl." He tucked in his chin to whisper, "Want to see your brother? He's sleeping, but you can take a peek."

She shook her head and didn't look. Quist did, though. He couldn't help it, any more than he could help looking at Lily again when he was done. She was beautiful, and she was the mother of his son. On top of all the other things he loved her for, he loved her for that.

In response to the exquisite look in his eyes, Lily touched his cheek. Then she gently rubbed Nicki's arm. "I've missed you so much, Nicki. I told the doctors that I had to go home tomorrow so that I could be with my daughter."

"How are you feeling?" Quist whispered.

She grinned and nodded, looked at Nicki, looked at the baby. "Incredible. I'm feeling incredible."

"How's he doing?"

She continued to grin. "Incredible." She slipped her thumb into Nicki's loose fist. The small fingers tightened around it. "But the food here is lousy. I miss our special superburgers with bacon."

"I had one yesterday," came the high little-girl voice.

"Did you?" Lily feigned hurt. "And you didn't bring one here for me?"

"I wanted to," Nicki said, "but Daddy said we should wait and make one when you get home." She turned her head just enough so that she could peek at Lily.

"I think I can live with that," Lily decided. "What else did Daddy make for you?"

"Fluff and popcorn and Chunky bars."

"Shhhh," Quist said. "You weren't supposed to tell her that."

Nicki giggled.

Lily loved it, but she didn't let on. "Quist, that's *terrible*. Fluff and popcorn and Chunky bars?"

"Not together," he argued, as though that would excuse it.

"You're corrupting this child."

"I like fluff," Nicki said. "And popcorn. And Chunky bars. Maybe baby wants a Chunky bar." She dared a glance at the infant.

"Mm, not for a little while, sweetheart. Babies only drink milk at the beginning."

"Did I?"

"Sure, you did." Lily had had the same conversation close to a dozen times with her daughter, but she didn't mind the repetition. Babies were something totally new for Nicki.

"His eyes are closed," the little girl said.

"He's sleeping. He'll do that a whole lot."

"When can I play with him?"

"When he's awake. Would you like that?"

She looked a little dubious, still she nodded.

"Come here," Lily said, and this time when she held out her arm, Nicki went right to her. When she was snuggled close to Lily's side, she reached out and timidly touched her brother's hand.

Lily smiled at Quist, who was smiling right back at her, and there were a myriad of messages going back and forth with those smiles.

Jonathan. I like the name Jonathan. After you. I like that, too.

They say he's perfect. Thank you for giving me a perfect son.

I'm glad it was a boy. Every man should have a son.

I'm glad we waited this long. We needed the time together, and Nicki needed the time with us.

Lord, do I love you, Quist.

Ah, Lily, you're the light of my life.

And the smiles went on.

COMING NEXT MONTH

CHRISTMAS IS FOR KIDS

Spend this holiday season with nine very special children. Children whose wishes come true at the magical time of Christmas.

Read American Romance's CHRISTMAS IS FOR KIDS—heartwarming holiday stories in which children bring together four couples who fall in love. Meet:

Frank, Dorcas, Kathy, Candy and Nicky—They become friends at St. Christopher's orphanage, but they really want to be adopted and become part of a real family, in #321 *A Carol Christmas* by Muriel Jensen.

Patty—She's a ten-year-old certified genius, but she wants what every little girl wishes for: a daddy of her own, in #322 *Mrs. Scrooge* by Barbara Bretton.

Amy and Flash—Their mom is about to deliver their newest sibling any day, but Christmas just isn't the same now—not without their dad. More than anything they want their family reunited for Christmas, in #323 *Dear Santa* by Margaret St. George.

Spencer—Living with his dad and grandpa in an all-male household has its advantages, but Spence wants Santa to bring him a mommy to love, in #324 *The Best Gift of All* by Andrea Davidson.

These children will win your hearts as they entice—and matchmake—the adults into a true romance. This holiday, invite them—and the four couples they bring together—into your home.

Look for all four CHRISTMAS IS FOR KIDS books available now from Harlequin American Romance. And happy holidays!

XMAS-KIDS-1R

Have You Ever Wondered If You Could Write A Harlequin Novel?

Here's great news—Harlequin is offering a series of cassette tapes to help you do just that. Written by Harlequin editors, these tapes give practical advice on how to make your characters—and your story—come alive. There's a tape for each contemporary romance series Harlequin publishes.

Mail order only

All sales final

TO: *Harlequin Reader Service*
Audiocassette Tape Offer
P.O. Box 1396
Buffalo, NY 14269-1396

I enclose a check/money order payable to HARLEQUIN READER SERVICE® for $9.70 ($8.95 plus 75¢ postage and handling) for EACH tape ordered for the total sum of $_____*
Please send:

☐ Romance and Presents   ☐ Intrigue
☐ American Romance   ☐ Temptation
☐ Superromance   ☐ All five tapes ($38.80 total)

Signature_____
                                        (please print clearly)
Name:_____

Address:_____

State:_____ Zip:_____

*Iowa and New York residents add appropriate sales tax.   AUDIO-H

Especially for you, Christmas from
HARLEQUIN HISTORICALS

An enchanting collection of three Christmas stories by some of your favorite authors captures the spirit of the season in the 1800s

TUMBLEWEED CHRISTMAS by Kristin James

A "Bah, humbug" Texas rancher meets his match in his new housekeeper, a woman determined to bring the spirit of a Tumbleweed Christmas into his life—and love into his heart.

A CINDERELLA CHRISTMAS by Lucy Elliot

The perfect granddaughter, sister and aunt, Mary Hillyer seemed destined for spinsterhood until Jack Gates arrived to discover a woman with dreams and passions that were meant to be shared during a Cinderella Christmas.

HOME FOR CHRISTMAS
by Heather Graham Pozzessere

The magic of the season brings peace Home For Christmas when a Yankee captain and a Southern heiress fall in love during the Civil War.

Look for HARLEQUIN HISTORICALS CHRISTMAS STORIES wherever Harlequin books are sold.

HIST-XMAS-1R

Wonderful, luxurious gifts can be yours with proofs-of-purchase from any specially marked ''Indulge A Little'' Harlequin or Silhouette book with the Offer Certificate properly completed, plus a check or money order (do not send cash) to cover postage and handling payable to Harlequin/Silhouette ''Indulge A Little, Give A Lot'' Offer. We will send you the specified gift.

Mail-in-Offer

OFFER CERTIFICATE

Item:	A. Collector's Doll	B. Soaps in a Basket	C. Potpourri Sachet	Đ. Scented Hangers
# of Proofs-of -Purchase	18	12	6	4
Postage & Handling	$3.25	$2.75	$2.25	$2.00
Check One				

Name _____

Address _____ Apt # _____

City _____ State _____ Zip _____

ONE PROOF OF PURCHASE

To collect your free gift by mail you must include the necessary number of proofs-of-purchase plus postage and handling with offer certificate.

HT-3

Harlequin®/Silhouette®

Mail this certificate, designated number of proofs-of-purchase and check or money order for postage and handling to:

INDULGE A LITTLE
P.O. Box 9055
Buffalo, N.Y. 14269-9055